CW00712968

'Do you live with him?' Yan cut in abruptly.

'No...' The proverbial tangled web, Eleanor thought as she evaded Yan's penetrating gaze.

'Are you sleeping with him?'

'That's none of your business!'

'You're not wearing an engagement ring,' Yan pointed out implacably.

'No. Not yet, but the engagement is semi-official...'

'Write him a letter,' Yan suggested indifferently. 'Tell him you are marrying the father of your child.'

'You're crazy! It would never work...'

Dear Reader

Whatever the weather this summer, come with us to four places in the sun. In this collection, we offer you the romance you love—with the Latin lovers of the Mediterranean...the colourful sights and sounds of Spain...the excitement and glamour of Venice...the natural beauty of Greece...the relaxed, timeless magic of France. A wonderful tour of sensual delight, with four happy endings along the way! Something sultry from Mills & Boon...

The Editor

Having abandoned her first intended career for marriage, **Rosalie Ash** spent several years as a bilingual personal assistant to the managing director of a leisure group. She now lives in Warwickshire with her husband, and daughters Kate and Abby, and her lifelong enjoyment of writing has led to her career as a novelist. Her interests include languages, travel and research for her books, reading, and visits to the Royal Shakespeare Theatre in nearby Stratford-upon-Avon. Other pleasures include swimming, yoga and country walks.

Recent titles by the same author:

CALYPSO'S ISLAND
ORIGINAL SIN
AN IMPORTED WIFE

APOLLO'S LEGEND

BY

ROSALIE ASH

All rights reserved. The text of this publication or any part thereof may not be reproduced or transmitted in any form or by any means, electronic or mechanical, including photocopying, recording, storage in an information retrieval system, or otherwise, without the written permission of the publisher.

This book is sold subject to the condition that it shall not, by way of trade or otherwise, be lent, re-sold, hired out or otherwise circulated without the prior consent of the publisher in any form of binding or cover other than that in which it is published and without a similar condition including this condition being imposed on the subsequent purchaser.

First published in Great Britain 1993
by Mills & Boon Limited

© Rosalie Ash 1993

Australian copyright 1993
Philippine copyright 1993
This edition 1993

ISBN 0 263 78518 1

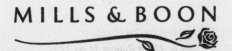

MILLS & BOON LIMITED
ETON HOUSE, 18-24 PARADISE ROAD
RICHMOND, SURREY TW9 1SR

The British Printing Company Ltd

All the characters in this book have no existence outside the imagination of the Author, and have no relation whatsoever to anyone bearing the same name or names. They are not even distantly inspired by any individual known or unknown to the Author, and all the incidents are pure invention.

All Rights Reserved. The text of this publication or any part thereof may not be reproduced or transmitted in any form or by any means, electronic or mechanical, including photocopying, recording, storage in an information retrieval system, or otherwise, without the written permission of the publisher.

This book is sold subject to the condition that it shall not, by way of trade or otherwise, be lent, resold, hired out or otherwise circulated without the prior consent of the publisher in any form of binding or cover other than that in which it is published and without a similar condition including this condition being imposed on the subsequent purchaser.

*First published in Great Britain 1994
by Mills & Boon Limited*

© Rosalie Ash 1994

*Australian copyright 1994
Philippine copyright 1994
This edition 1994*

ISBN 0 263 78518 1

*Set in Times Roman 11 on 12 pt.
86-9407-48526 C*

*Printed in Great Britain by
BPC Paperbacks Ltd
A member of
The British Printing Company Ltd*

CHAPTER ONE

How dared he? How *dared* he? The furious litany had been going round and round in her head for the last twenty-four agonising, unbearable hours. Of course, she'd always known that Yan Diamakis considered himself to be the modern equivalent of a Greek god, that he inhabited an alien world, where male supremacy went relatively unchallenged. This knowledge had been one of the many reasons why their brief, doomed relationship had crashed.

But even so, she'd never in ten million years have thought him capable of this. Of stealing Christophor, of kidnapping her little three-year-old son and disappearing back to Greece like this...

Dashing a shaky hand across her eyes, Eleanor bit back a sting of angry tears. Suitcase in hand, she emerged from the crowded chaos of Skiathos Airport in July, and gazed almost unseeingly at the equal chaos outside. Queues of perspiring holiday-makers were visibly wilting as they disembarked from transfer buses. She looked bleakly around for a taxi. The heat of the little pine-clad island hit her like an open oven door, after the brief cool of the air-conditioned building.

She blinked determinedly, swallowing the choked emotion back into her throat. It was devastating, being back here. The memories were crushing in on her with the familiar sounds, sights and smells of the island. But tears were a weakness she couldn't afford. She couldn't show any more weakness. Her letter to Yan had been weakness. She realised that now. She'd thought it showed maturity, showed strength of character, compassion maybe...but you couldn't reason with someone like Yan Diamakis...

'Thessa Beach Hotel, please,' she told the taxi driver, sitting back in the rear seat of the dusty Mercedes, and drawing a deep breath. She didn't intend pulling any punches. If it hadn't been for Christophor, she wouldn't have dreamed of marching straight into the Diamakis hotel and bearding the proverbial lion in his den. But she felt as fierce as a lioness protecting her young. In snatching Christophor, Yan had committed a crime she would find it very hard to forgive...and cold fury was a very effective antidote to fear...

The road twisted and wound its way along the south coast, with pot-holes and deep, uneven cambers, revealing dizzy drops into bite-shaped bays, and sloping green mountains to the north. Not even the familiar breakneck panache of the Sciathan taxi-drivers, or the suicidal islanders' habit of roaring along the centre of the road, could distract her from her burning commitment to see justice done.

And yet...the island was so beautiful. It was no place to be feeling violently vengeful, or seethingly indignant. Flowers dazzled the eye in every direction. Flame-red hibiscus, hot-pink bougainvillaea, pink and white oleander. Beneath their red-pantiled roofs, the houses had a blinding chalk-white symmetry against the impossible blue of the sky.

This small, northerly Greek island had captured her heart four years ago, and its fairy-tale spell was still alive. Eleanor pushed back her hair, a long, heavy swath of shiny nut-brown, and relaxed sufficiently to sniff the breeze reluctantly through the open car window. Resin and juniper needles, and wild thyme. A warm, sensual mixture which stirred and lifted the spirits. Even spirits as tormented and shattered as hers.

The taxi screeched to an abrupt halt in a cloud of dust at the end of the dirt-track leading down to the hotel, and she stepped shakily out of the car as the driver went to retrieve her suitcase from the boot. The scratch and shrill of crickets in the somnolent late afternoon sounded almost as loud as the bleeping of a telephone signal.

'*Efharisto*,' she murmured wryly, handing over a wad of drachmas, including a tip, and bracing herself for the short walk to Yan's hotel.

'*Parakalo*!' The formal courtesy came automatically, but the driver flashed her an appreciative grin, swiftly assessing Eleanor's appearance, from brilliant blue-green eyes and stubbornly square chin, to long shapely legs in white cotton-drill bermudas. 'Enjoy your holiday!'

If he only knew, Eleanor reflected, turning stiffly away to begin the walk down towards the beach. This was about as far as she could get from an enjoyable holiday. This could be the beginning of a nightmare...

Four years ago she'd felt free as the wind, riding her perilous little moped along this very same track towards that same wedge of sapphire sea. It had been her very first season as a tour representative for a holiday company, in Skiathos. She'd been loving every minute of her job, enjoying the warm, friendly Greek hospitality, the beautiful island. Everything had seemed uncomplicated, and perfectly planned. The complication she couldn't possibly have foreseen was meeting Yan, taking one stunned look at him, and falling—no, *imagining* she was falling—hopelessly in love with him...

She'd reached the end of the dirt-track. To the left was the hotel, etched into the hillside, its gardens sloping lushly down to the pale sand of the beach. Tall pine trees grew right down to the sand. Holiday-makers splashed in the still blue sea, or dozed on striped beach-beds beneath white sun umbrellas.

Even though it was July, the beach wasn't crowded. This was a private beach, the hotel's own, and their charge for beach-beds and parasols tended to keep the crowds at bay.

Eleanor caught her breath abruptly. Maybe she was just so charged up with emotion, maybe motherhood equipped women with some extra-sensory perception, but she could swear that was Christophor down near the sea...

Her heart thudding, she dropped her suitcase where she stood, and shielded her eyes against the brilliance of the afternoon sun. Down near the water's edge stood a very small boy, wearing bright red and white striped swimming-trunks. Thick straight hair, dark as a rook's wing, blew in the steady off-shore breeze. The child turned slightly, thumb in mouth, presenting a grave, solemn, adorable profile so familiar and so dear to Eleanor that she gave it no more debate. Springing to life, she raced down across the soft, hot sand, calling Christophor's name. Closer still, and the relief and joy blotted out everything else as recognition dawned in the child's eyes, and he yelled 'Mummy' with almost as much passion as Eleanor's broken greeting.

Cradling Christophor in her arms, she sank to the sand, uncaring of the surprised glances from those near by. She wasn't sure which was the strongest emotion: joy that her son was safe, that he was *here*, just as Yan's cryptic note had said he would be, or fierce anger that he'd been taken from her without permission.

'Mummy!' The delight in Christophor's voice was almost tangible. As was his evident contentment. 'Do you like our surprise holiday? Papa *said* you would come today!'

'Did he?' With superhuman control, Eleanor kept her voice light and level. 'Where is Papa now, Christophor? Don't tell me he's left you down here on the beach on your own.'

'No, Eleanor. He has not.'

Eleanor went very still, fighting down the shivers, fighting to get her breathing under control.

Silly to let something as basic as a man's voice get under her skin, every single time she heard it. It wasn't even as if this were the first time in four years that she'd seen him.

She'd overcome that trauma a few days earlier.
He'd responded to her letter by materialising at the
hotel where she worked, in Northumberland, within
a few days of her dropping the envelope in a red
letter-box in the village, and wondering if she'd
done the right thing...

'Well? Aren't you going to say hello?' The
fathoms-deep, indescribably masculine voice compelled her to lift her head and acknowledge his
presence.

'Hello, Yan.'

'Hello, Eleanor.'

The silence seemed louder than the deafening
shrill of the crickets. With Christophor shielded in
her arms, Eleanor felt abruptly oblivious to her
surroundings, to people around them. Her little
son, as he wriggled closer against her, felt cool from
a recent dip in the sea. The sea-water on the red-
striped swim trunks was dampening Eleanor's
shorts and her brief, sleeveless turquoise T-shirt.
But all Eleanor was really aware of was the nearness
of Yan Diamakis, towering over her as she knelt in
the sand, putting her at an instant disadvantage,
exuding a powerful aura of cool confrontation.

'I hope you weren't too worried. My note was
clear, *ne*?'

'Yes. Your note was clear.' Eleanor cleared her
husky throat, and fought down the insidious ache
inside her. She was so angry with him that it was
surely impossible to feel such a surge of physical
and emotional attraction? She blinked up at him,
the sun in her eyes. 'We need to talk,' she added,
icy determination in her voice. 'Alone.'

The black eyes, long and cat-like, narrowed mockingly. Yan was over six feet tall and built like a Greek god, despite his English ancestry through his mother. He was darkly tanned and radiating good health, and, in brief but well-cut black swimming-trunks, no detail of his physical perfection went unnoticed. He possessed the enviable pectorals, the sloping well-honed shoulders, the washboard abdomen and long, muscled thighs of Adonis himself.

But, as Eleanor reminded herself defensively, his classic male beauty fell just short of perfection. His strong nose had been broken at some point in his past. Perhaps by someone as simmeringly furious with him as she was now? And the firm mouth was just a touch too wide, the cynical lines from nostril to mouth too deeply entrenched. Minor points, true. But enough to make him comfortably a member of the human race, instead of some mythical reincarnation . . .

Eleanor felt her anger flare, uncontrollably. Why did the wretched man always have to look as if life were one long joke? How could he still be so . . . so sexually compelling, so meltingly gorgeous? How *dared* he look like that, so . . . confident and *amused* . . . when he'd just kidnapped her baby son, abducted him illegally to Greece, on some arrogant whim?

'Are you not afraid to be alone with me, Eleanor?' he taunted softly. As he spoke he dropped to his haunches, aiming a charm-charged smile at Christophor. To Eleanor's chagrin, Christophor solemnly removed his thumb and thoughtfully rewarded Yan with a brilliant smile in return. The Greeks' love of children was all-consuming, she recalled bitterly. That fact in itself didn't excuse Yan's actions in stealing Christophor, but it went a small way to explaining it, she knew. Laura, a fellow rep with a lot more experience than Eleanor, and a confidently outspoken personality, had bluntly warned her that once Yan knew that Christophor was his he would stop at nothing to keep him in Greece . . .

But maybe, after what she'd done four years ago, Yan had the right to be blazingly angry with her . . .

'*Afraid* to be alone with you?' Eleanor cut in with a bravery she was suddenly far from feeling. 'Not in the least! Stop imagining you're so irresistible no female is safe in your company!'

'But I do not think that.' The retort was guarded, the dark face unreadable as he scanned her tense features. 'This has always been in your imagination. This vision of me as the great seducer of women . . .'

'No . . .'

'Yes, I think so.' Yan made a decisive movement with his head which made her think of an eagle coldly assessing its victim. 'After all, if I am so irresistible, why did you run away from me, Eleanor?'

There was a trace of rough, banked-down emotion in the deep voice. It touched a buried chord deep inside her which flinched from reminders. In a secret turmoil inside now, she clutched Christophor a little tighter, and felt her small son wriggle in protest.

'You know why I left,' she managed at last. 'And I don't imagine anything has changed...'

There was a heavy silence. Yan's dark gaze was intent, but she avoided his eyes, gazing sightlessly across the beach, battling against the weight of the past. Abruptly, she couldn't bear her treacherous responses to his closeness a second longer. She stood up, lifting Christophor with her.

Yan straightened up too, in a swift, effortless spring. Eleanor wasn't over-tall. Even when she stiffly drew herself up to her full five feet five inches, Yan had the impressive advantage in height. And now, with a faint stirring of apprehension, she noticed the coldly determined light in his eyes, despite the smile he had for Christophor.

'Everything has changed,' he informed her with ominous calm. 'It changed the moment your letter arrived.'

'Papa...!' Christophor held out small plump hands towards him, without warning, and when Yan coolly reached to lift him into his arms he went, snuggling against him. Eleanor watched helplessly, her stomach contracting in panic, and mounting fury. Denial in her heart, all she could do was gaze speechlessly at the sight of father and tiny son, so physically alike, so blatantly happy in each other's company...

'How *could* you be so cruel, Yan?' she heard herself blurt out, too overcome to restrain herself any longer for Christophor's sake. 'How could you have taken him like that, tricked me like that, put me through this hell...?'

'You will achieve nothing by hurling accusations at me. And you, of all people, should know all there is to know about *trickery*,' he rasped abruptly, retrieving a T-shirt and jeans from a nearby sunbed, and gesturing to Eleanor to follow him. 'Come. We will go up to my private house, and we will talk. Just as you request . . .'

'Big of you,' she muttered through her teeth. With a fresh shudder of anguish, she stalked after him. Christophor's large dark eyes, unnervingly the colour of Yan's, watched her contentedly over Yan's shoulder. Even their hair was identical. Thick, dark, straight, shining with clean, glossy good health. Christophor, normally so reserved and wary, so grave and slow to respond to strangers, already besotted with his father? Retrieving her suitcase from where she'd dropped it a few minutes earlier, Eleanor had to restrain a reprehensible urge to aim a furious kick at Yan's departing back . . .

Yan's private house, a new acquisition since her spell here four years ago, proved to be a low, rambling old white villa a short drive around the bay, through silvery olive groves. Emerging from the dusty open-top jeep a few minutes later, Eleanor realised that this place, like the hotel, had gardens which reached down to the beach, shady with pine and cypress and juniper. Except that this beach, unlike the one by the hotel, appeared to be a completely private affair, a tiny melon-slice inlet of shimmering white sand just a short walk around the headland from the hotel's beach, with a white motor-launch reflecting the sun in a blinding reflection against the dark blue sea.

'You were lucky to see us on the hotel beach, among the crowds,' Yan murmured casually as he led the way beneath the welcome shade of a bamboo awning.

'Mothers have natural radar where their babies are concerned,' Eleanor said through gritted teeth. Sitting down on the proffered cane chair, she suddenly realised how hot and tired she felt. Lifting a shaking hand to her face, she rubbed her eyes wearily. The last few days had been draining, emotionally, physically, mentally. It was too late to go back, wipe out that foolish urge to appease her conscience, blot out that letter to Yan. Imagine... *imagine* thinking that time could heal the tension! That she and Yan Diamakis could sit down together as sane, rational human beings and work out a solution to this mess they'd got themselves into...

But when he'd appeared at Aunt Meg's rambling country house hotel in Northumberland, awesomely tall, dark and powerful in expensive grey suit and immaculate white silk shirt, all the conflicting feelings of the past had rushed back with devastating force. Just seeing him again had been traumatic. Instantly recalling every intimate moment, every intense, passionate longing she'd ever felt for him. Remembering how desperately she'd yearned for his love...

It had meant that her intentions to be calm, sane and reasonable had vanished within seconds. His request to take Christophor on a visit to Greece with him had made her heart clench with fear, and fear had made her refusal instantaneous, a reflex self-defence...

So he'd tricked her. Or rather tricked Karen, the girl who helped with Christophor while Eleanor managed the leisure, health and beauty facilities at the hotel. Yan had announced his intention to take his little son for an outing, strapped him into a hired baby seat in his hired Mercedes, then calmly driven to Newcastle Airport and disappeared back here to Skiathos with him...

'What would you like to drink, Eleanor?' Yan's cool voice cut in on her thoughts. She looked up to see that a dark-haired, smiling, middle-aged woman had appeared on the terrace—presumably Yan's housekeeper.

'Coffee, please.' It felt an effort to speak.

'Thank you, Evangelie. I will have coffee too. And could you take Christophor and give him a drink and biscuit?'

Yan's voice was wry as he glanced at Eleanor's white, set face. Restraining herself from launching dementedly to retrieve her baby merited a medal, Eleanor decided. But Christophor seemed quite happy to be placed gently on his feet, willingly holding out his hand to go with Evangelie. Far from the bundle of nerves and insecurity Eleanor had feared, Christophor appeared to have survived his kidnapping ordeal without visible scars. In fact he actually seemed to be *enjoying* himself. As if this were all some marvellous game...

If a three-year-old could cope with the situation, surely at the advanced age of twenty-five *she* could cope? Hands clenched in her lap, she worked desperately for poise and detachment.

'So you found my note,' Yan mused expressionlessly when they were finally alone on the terrace. 'And the air ticket. And you came, just as I intended you should. Stop looking at me as if I am the worst species of child-thief, Eleanor. Christophor is happy here. He knows I am his father. Obviously he has missed having a father until now. I rather think he likes the idea.'

Reading the triumphant gleam in his dark eyes, her good intentions of calm and reason yet again vanished without trace.

'You . . . *bastard*!' she whispered shakily, glaring at him with such fierce resentment that she saw the glint of battle intensify in his eyes. He'd donned the clothes he'd retrieved from the beach, and in the black T-shirt and khaki jeans he looked unbearably attractive as well as formidably determined. He leaned lazily back in his chair.

'Because of *your* actions,' he said curtly, 'it is our child who is the bastard, Eleanor. Not me.'

'I thought I'd stopped hating you. Now I can see that I've only just begun!'

'Why whisper?' he mocked. 'Why not shout your insults out loud, Eleanor?'

'If we were really alone, I would! But with Christophor within hearing distance, and your housekeeper hovering near by, I think maybe you're the one who's afraid to be alone with *me*.'

'You're not making much sense.' Abruptly he stood up, and caught hold of her wrist, pulling her up too. 'But if you want to be entirely alone with me, that is not a problem.'

Speechless, her wrist burning from the touch of his hand, she found herself hauled inside the house, and into a large upstairs bedroom. Dark maroon, navy and sand décor proclaimed masculine ownership. The heavy oak door was snapped decisively shut and locked behind them, and Yan leaned against the door, releasing her, watching her through narrowed dark eyes.

'All right, Eleanor. Shout. Fight. Insult me,' he taunted cruelly. 'Let out all that pent-up fury before you explode in a shower of venom.'

She was shaking from head to toe.

'You'd rather I burst into tears, wouldn't you?' she whispered raggedly. 'You're so sadistic, you would *love* to see me weeping and begging, is that it?'

'Am I sadistic?' He took a step towards her, and she steeled herself not to flinch away. 'Is it not you who are sadistic? To fool me into believing you had lost our baby? Fool me into believing you had miscarried at an early stage? Just so you could break off our engagement to marry, run away back to England, and hide my child from me?'

There was a ring of icy fury in his voice now.

'That's typical of you!' she breathed, shaking her head frantically as he moved closer. 'Don't you see? That's one reason I had to leave! It terrified me, this... this obsession with *your* child! With your child having to stay here in Greece! The child was all you cared about! The sheer *arrogance* of it, Yan, when it was *my* child, growing inside *me*...'

She got no further. With a rough curse he took the last stride to close the space between them and dragged her against him with savage lack of finesse. Rigidly defiant, she froze like a statue as he crushed her hard against his chest.

'Yan, don't——' she began furiously, but then her words were cut off as he snaked a hand up to the nape of her neck and jerked her head painfully back, his fingers tangling in the long, shiny brown of her hair.

'Don't what?' he rasped thickly. 'In hell's name, Eleanor, I hardly trust myself with you...'

She opened her mouth to defend herself, and as she did so he dropped his head and covered her lips with his.

The kiss was ferocious. A taming, invading, devastating assault on her pride. But then a heat swept through her as the kiss softened, growing in hunger and desire, threatening to consume her in its flames. Worst of all was the powerful flare of response Eleanor detected inside herself.

Writhing frantically in his grip, she fought to deny it. This was dreadful. One kiss igniting a volatile bush-fire, after years fighting to extinguish it?

Catching her breath involuntarily, she longed to arch against him, to close her eyes and let her fingers move yearningly over the flat, athletic muscles of his shoulders, the hard plane of his back. But the dire consequences of such surrender gave her the strength to kick and fight. Somehow she managed to push him away, gasping for breath, her pulses racing.

'Stop it!' she stormed at him, glaring at his grimly amused expression. 'What do you think you're proving? Simply that you're *stronger* than me? I suppose next you'll prove what a big, strong man you are by hitting me.'

'I've proved that you still want me, Eleanor.' There was an implacable note of certainty in his voice.

His cool arrogance sent her temper soaring even higher. Humiliated, she lashed at him blindly. The blow was neatly fenced. With a muffled shriek she lost her balance, falling backwards. The wide double bed cushioned her fall, but she found herself in the ignominious position of being pinned there by her wrists.

'You cannot accuse me of attacking you,' he pointed out with a twinge of dark humour.

She could feel his eyes on her body, roaming down over the rapid rise and fall of her breasts and focusing with lazy intensity on her tightening nipples, pressing hard against the soft fabric of her T-shirt. This had ridden up in the tussle, and the breeze from the ceiling fan cooled her hot abdomen in the gap above the waistband of her white shorts. Almost thoughtfully he moved his hand to stroke that exposed area of flesh, contouring the arch of her narrow waist, the indent of her navel.

His expert touch sent an involuntary clenching shudder through her stomach.

'Still beautiful, Eleanor,' he murmured, his gaze suddenly grimmer, his breathing a touch more ragged as he inspected the smooth firmness of her stomach beneath the jut of her ribcage. 'Still perfect in every way. Even if you'd had stretch marks and sagging muscles, you would have been beautiful. But there is none...'

He bent to kiss her trembling lips, his eyes velvet-dark beneath heavy lids. 'Admit it,' he taunted softly, his caress moving higher to brush the tell-tale points of her breasts as she shivered convulsively beneath the intimacy. 'Admit you still feel something for me.'

'I can't think what I *ever* found attractive about you!' she choked at him in desperation. Inside she was dying, melting, burning up with wanting him...

'No?' Abruptly, with a brief laugh, he released her wrists and straightened up. 'I can. You were eloquent about it at the time, as I recall...'

'Yan, for pity's sake!' Sitting up unsteadily, she hauled her T-shirt down, balling her fists at her sides.

'Remember Daphne and Apollo?' He grinned down at her mercilessly. She winced at his goading reminder of her fascination with Greek mythology, her light-hearted game of drawing parallels in their own relationship... 'Only you had the legend mixed up. You forgot that Daphne ran away from Apollo *before* he could take her virginity. She didn't wait until he'd impregnated her with a little baby god before vanishing into hiding, Eleanor!'

'How you can *joke* about all this I can't imagine!'

'No. You're right. It's not funny, is it?'

There was a fraught, charged silence suddenly. Crossing her arms defensively, she tried to control the frantic thudding of her heart. She wanted to stand up, but she wasn't sure her legs would hold her weight.

'All you ever cared about was sex,' she said with soft bitterness. 'If I hadn't been so young and stupid I'd have realised that!'

'At twenty-five you still don't know all the answers, even now, Eleanor. Has it occurred to you that you might still have your facts mixed up?'

'No!'

'At least I know where my responsibilities lie,' he countered drily. 'And if you're worried I'm going to ravish you all over again, you can relax.' His tone was caustic as he eyed her tense position. 'I will try to contain my *base* desires. At least, until we are man and wife.'

'*What*?' The word was jerked from her lips so violently that it shook her whole body.

'I think you heard what I said, Eleanor.' The soft arrogance in his voice brought a surge of hot colour to her cheeks.

'Yan, surely...' Her voice croaked on a dry throat. She stopped, got unsteadily to her feet. Her heart was hammering so hard that it felt as if it might burst. 'Surely even you cannot be so...so thick-skinned, you imagine I'd ever marry you?'

'It is perhaps *you* who are thick-skinned,' he retorted easily. 'Tell me, what did you *think* would happen when you wrote that letter to me, Eleanor?'

'I explained in the letter!' Her voice rose a fraction, husky with frustration and fear. 'I felt you had a right to know about Christophor. That's all...'

'That's *all*? You thought I had a right to know that I have a son? Three years too late?' Yan was restraining his temper with monumental control, she realised. 'Now don't you think I have the *right* to legitimise my son's birth?'

Eleanor drew a deep, ragged breath.

'The only thing that matters to me is to make sure Christophor grows up in a calm, loving environment...' she began, with as much cool confidence as she could muster.

'And so he will.' Yan's voice was ruthlessly decisive as he turned towards the door. 'Follow me. I will show you where you are to sleep. And remember this. Christophor is *my* son. Taking him back to England is not an option, Eleanor. His home—and therefore *your* home—is here. In Greece.'

The hard set of Yan's face as he ushered her with elaborate courtesy out of the door seemed even more ominous than his words.

CHAPTER TWO

IT WASN'T really surprising, Eleanor thought bleakly, that she couldn't sleep. It was ridiculous to feel like the victim in some Hans Christian Andersen fairy-tale, locked up in an ivory tower awaiting some monstrous fate. And yet leaning here on the rail of the small balcony outside her bedroom, watching the pearly path of the moon on the black Aegean Sea, with the shrill song of the crickets tautening her nerves to screaming point, she felt suspended in time and space, as if anything could happen . . .

In spite of the warmth of the night, she shivered in her cream satin slip. She could hear the murmur of the wind in the pine trees. It was an eerie, lonely sound. It seemed to emphasise her isolation. Abruptly, once the wary affair of dinner was over, and Evangelie, in spite of Eleanor's protests, was consigned to supervise Christophor's bath and bedtime, she'd realised how alone she felt.

There was Aunt Meg, of course, back in Northumberland. She'd been the one who'd finally triggered Eleanor's confession to Yan. But she had her hotel to supervise, and could hardly be expected to arbitrate between Yan and herself. Both her parents were dead. She'd never known her father. He'd left her mother for another woman, shortly after Eleanor was born.

When her mother had died too, about ten years ago, Eleanor had gone to live with Aunt Meg until leaving school to pursue her career in tourism. She'd lived in a bed-sit in London for three years, before taking up her first foreign posting. After the fiasco of her relationship with Yan Diamakis, her aunt's country hotel in Northumberland had been a ready-made haven, whereabouts unknown to Yan...

Clasping her arms round herself, she gnawed her lip distractedly, memories of that fateful summer nudging back to torment her...

Arriving in Skiathos as an inexperienced representative, Eleanor had found herself sharing lodgings with Laura. Five years her senior, Laura had travelled the world as a tour rep, done everything, seen everything, and seemed very over-protective, over-zealous about Eleanor's welfare. She'd given her a stern lecture about the perils of the local male population, and, although she'd been powerless to do anything but stand by and watch when Eleanor fell head over heels in love with Yan Diamakis, it had been her well-meaning interference that had brought it all to crisis-point...

Eleanor winced when she remembered how totally, how instantly, she'd been afflicted by that 'love at first sight' thunderbolt. Thessa Beach Hotel was where Laura had called regularly to greet new parties of holiday-makers. As the representative of the tour operators, she had known the Diamakis family, the hotel's owners. She'd given Eleanor a quick potted history of the family. How the hotel had been built on land owned by the Diamakis clan, how it had been run with grace, flair and enthusiasm by Yan's mother, an Englishwoman much younger than her Greek husband. She'd wryly mentioned the dynamic, sexually magnetic son, who'd sidelined a successful career in shipping and air freight to come over from Athens to help his ageing father run the hotel, following his mother's tragic death.

Yan, Laura had pronounced cheerfully, was the kind of male to avoid at all costs. Suave, sophisticated, worldly-wise, and highly dangerous to any female over the age of sixteen.

Eleanor met him on the beach, during her free time. It was early in the evening, still sunny, but quieter, the hour when most holiday-makers had left the beach to get ready for their evening out. Eleanor had walked down from the village, in the cooler evening air, and had sat down on one of the deserted beach-beds to watch the never-ending plying of boats and ferries, fishing caiques and hydrofoils, which were a constant feature of the waters around the Greek islands.

There was someone water-skiing, way out in the turquoise sweep of the bay. This clearly wasn't one of the inexperienced tourists, collapsing into the waves every ten yards. Roaring along in the wake of a powerful speedboat was a man who obviously knew every trick in the book. He looked relaxed and casual, skiing one-armed, one-legged, weaving and swerving, laughing with the driver ahead, the golden evening sun glinting off a glorious, darkly tanned torso and strong, muscular limbs. If he'd been putting on a show for the earlier crowds, she'd have decided he was showing off. But the beach was virtually deserted. He was doing it for himself, revelling in his enjoyment of the sport . . .

Eleanor watched enviously. Men like that made it look so easy. As the speedboat arced back in towards the beach the skier smoothly crested into the shallows, at high speed, and somehow managed to finish up slicing, upright, straight on to the sand without losing his balance.

Open-mouthed, she watched this vision of masculine perfection in brief black swimming-trunks wave and shout something to the speedboat driver, grab a white towel from the sand, then sprint up the beach towards the hotel. This *had* to be the professional water-ski instructor, she decided, taking time out to practise his skills and enjoy himself now that the official business of the day was over. His direction brought him close to where she sat, and, catching sight of her fixed gaze and round-eyed admiration, he slowed down, and grinned at her in a friendly way.

'*Kalispera, thespinis.*'

'Could you teach me to do that?' she queried bluntly.

He laughed out loud. 'Personally?' he queried, that deep voice tinged with the teasing note she was to come to know so well.

'Well, yes. Of course.' A touch of irritation tinged her voice. 'How much do you charge?'

One dark eyebrow had lifted a fraction. Eleanor found herself the subject of a leisurely, amused appraisal by the darkest, most unnerving gaze she'd ever seen. Starting with her thick mane of shiny brown hair, and brilliant, translucent green-blue eyes, moving to the innocently sexy fullness of her mouth, the stubborn squareness of her jaw, the cool male inspection then roamed lower to the high jut of young breasts and narrow, flat waist and stomach beneath a smoky-blue Lycra swimsuit and washed-out denim shorts.

'For you, *thespinis*, lessons would be free of charge,' he assured her gravely.

'Oh, I certainly couldn't accept——'

'*Parakalo,*' he said with a twitch of laughter on his lips. 'Please. It will be my pleasure.'

'Well, if you're quite sure.' Suddenly acutely self-conscious beneath that sardonic gaze, she stood up, thrusting her hands into her pockets, thinking rapidly about her next free spell. 'My name's Eleanor Carrington. Could I come . . . tomorrow?'

'At this time?' he suggested calmly.

'All right. It's a deal,' she said with an effort at airy nonchalance. 'And thanks . . . *efharisto.*'

'*Parakalo.*' The wry response was accompanied by a cool nod, and then he walked on past her in the direction of the hotel, a lithe, loping walk, without a backward glance . . .

He let her go on thinking he was the ski instructor for a whole fortnight. Any laughter or joking remarks between the speedboat driver and her 'instructor' were conducted in rapid, softly guttural Greek. Eleanor remained unaware of her mistake. Under his expert tuition, she progressed with relative ease from floundering novice to reasonable proficiency. But as the days went by it was her mounting physical attraction to him that developed faster than her prowess on water-skis.

From the first tingling touch of his fingers on her bare shoulders and thighs, as he'd shown her the correct crouching start-position in the shallows, she'd been gripped by a nameless desire, stronger than any emotion she'd ever encountered in all her twenty-one years.

Yan had no idea, or so she thought. She fought to hide the flare of response she felt inside, averting her eyes quickly from his if his gaze seemed too searching, affecting a casual, nonchalant air whenever they talked together. This warm, honeyed ache in her stomach, this trembling feeling in her thighs, this sudden spurt in her pulse-rate whenever he shot her one of his swift, approving grins... It confused her, made her feel vulnerable and self-conscious. Tossing from side to side in bed each night, she painfully analysed her jumbled emotions and realised she must be suffering from a gigantic infatuation, all the more unnerving because of this new physical arousal he'd triggered. Until then, Eleanor's experience of men had been limited to clumsy kisses or groping caresses at parties with boys of her own age. Not one of them had managed to overcome her basic belief that her body was her own, private possession, not to be meddled with by anyone else. Yet now, without so much as a single kiss, without a single caress, she was trembling with need.

And it wasn't just a physical longing. It was deeply emotional too. Her heart leapt when she saw him lounging against the boats, talking with the driver, waiting for her. Her emotions nosedived if she arrived before him and feared he wouldn't turn up.

She developed an acute awareness of time and place, a heightened appreciation of her surroundings. The sky just before the sun began to sink, as late as nine o'clock, still light but fading fast. The pale misty grey of the sea as it merged with the darkening sky. The long blurred outline of the island of Euboea across the water, turning a ghostly milky-white. The apricot sunset in the west. The sharpening scent of wild thyme, and honeysuckle, and juniper. She walked around in a rosy-pink bubble of elation, unpredictable, subject to sudden violent mood swings. She was in love, for the very first time. Deeply, secretly, hopelessly in love with this tall mocking stranger who was teaching her to water-ski...

It was Laura who first spotted the deception.

'What in the *world* are you doing, meeting Yan Diamakis every other night for water-skiing lessons?' she demanded, widening round hazel eyes and shaking back her short auburn curls in astonishment. Eleanor's blank expression spoke volumes. Armed with the truth, and quivering with illogical rage, she met him on the beach that evening and let forth a torrent of pent-up frustration. Why hadn't he told her he was the hotel owner? Why had he fooled her he was the water-ski instructor? Just to amuse himself at her expense? Well, he could *stick* his water-skiing lessons in an unmentionable place, as far as she was concerned. And if he let her know what she owed the real water-ski school, she'd be more than happy to settle her debts...

The torrent was stilled by Yan's husky laugh, then by the ungovernable surge of reaction as he pulled her gently into his arms and kissed her, for the very first time.

Something magical seemed to happen then, something which seemed to Eleanor to embrace every wildly romantic fairy-tale she'd ever read. The kiss felt right, familiar, yet frighteningly strange. The abrupt flare of need in them both brought them crushed into each other's arms, clutching each other in silent surprise.

'Eleanor...Eleanor...' The deep, infinitely beautiful timbre of Yan's voice sounded like a benediction as he drew away a fraction, scanned her stunned face with darkening eyes, then pulled her close again. In the scant covering of swimwear, this intimate meeting of bodies was triggering a devastating reaction. Heat mounted, zigzagged between them like lightning ricocheting off the surface of the sea. With a choked sob she clung to his broad shoulders, shivering and trembling as he gently steered her away from the grinning speedboat driver and led her back up the beach into the relative privacy of the pine trees. There was a beach-bed, pulled up into the trees by someone seeking shade from the midday sun. Yan sat Eleanor down here, and came down beside her, his eyes ruefully amused as he took stock of the situation.

'*Se thélo*, Eleanor,' he told her in a deep, wry, hoarse voice, 'I want you. So badly, I am burning

inside. Forgive me, *agapití mou*. Normally I am a
man well in control of my....physical desires. With
you...' He tailed off, sketching an imaginary explosion in the air with his hands.

'Don't...' Eleanor's voice let her down. She tried
again, gripping Yan's strong, lean hands tightly in
hers. 'Don't apologise. I...feel the same way...'

The dark eyebrow tilted with a trace of mockery,
despite Yan's evident emotional state. 'How old are
you, Eleanor?'

'Twenty-one. Fully adult. Old enough to know
my own mind...' What was she saying? The words
came without conscious thought.

'And I am thirty-one. Old enough to resist such
urges if I know them to be unwise,' he countered,
huskily rueful. 'I think perhaps I should hand you
over to the *real* watersports school, for lessons of
a less dangerous kind...'

'I don't need any more lessons,' she told him in
a low, choked voice. 'I've learned all I need to
know...' Naïve, unthinking, she shyly reached and
touched the warm, hard muscle of his thigh, and
after a brief instant of frozen resistance she was
rewarded by the shudder of fierce answering need
in Yan as he folded her against him. In the shadow
of the pine trees, they lingered there on the beach-
bed, kissing with mounting hunger and urgency,
until the sky turned a dark Prussian blue, and the
hotel gardens were bathed in floodlights.

Later they had dinner together in an intimate little
taverna in Skiathos Town. Laura was out when
Eleanor was showering and dressing, but although
she had imagined her friend's cynical warnings her

feelings for Yan were too strong, too overwhelming, to be ignored. When Yan appeared to
collect her, in a black open-top jeep, she emerged
radiant in a swirly sea-green silk two-piece, shoe-
string straps and calf-length skirt giving her a de-
liciously feminine feeling which intensified as the
evening progressed.

Yan as a watersports instructor was powerfully
attractive. Yan as a dinner companion, cool,
urbane, witty, charming, every inch the rich Athens
shipping magnate and wealthy respected hotel
owner, in cream silk shirt and impeccably tailored
tan silk suit, was utterly devastating.

They talked about everything there was to talk
about, or so it seemed to Eleanor. Their past, families, taste in spicy food, Greek myths and ancient
history, poetry, rock music and Impressionist art,
her brief indecision between art school or the tourist
industry as a career, his mother's love of art, having
taught the subject before her marriage . . .

It felt like talking with an old friend. Someone
who understood her, someone she barely knew but
who appeared to be miraculously on her wave-
length. She couldn't ever remember feeling so good
in someone else's company. Her previous life
seemed like a grey, one-dimensional backdrop. The
only vivid reality, sharp and colourful and painfully alive, was now, sitting in the warm night air
on the old harbour front, sharing food and wine
and conversation with Yan.

When the restaurant part of the evening came to
a close, a nightclub in the town seemed the only
option. Moving on there after the meal, she plunged

ever deeper into the tangled web of sexual desire
and emotional need. Dancing with Yan brought
goose-bumps to her freshly tanned skin, made her
knees shake and crumple underneath her. The heat
from his body warmed her deep inside. She felt faint
with nervous tension.

When they finally climbed back into the jeep, in
the early hours of the morning, Yan tipped up her
chin and searched her flushed face. His eyes looked
shadowy, velvet-black with suppressed desire.

'Eleanor... sweet, innocent little Eleanor...' It
was half-tease, half-groan. He cupped her face with
both hands, his touch a fraction unsteady. 'Did your
mother never tell you not to look at a man like
that?'

'She probably would have done,' she admitted
with a short laugh. The only lasting advice she could
recall from her rather embittered mother was never
to marry without love, a detail she felt somehow
unsuitable for passing on to Yan Diamakis on such
short acquaintance. 'But she died when I was
fifteen. My colleague Laura lectures me on a regular
basis, though!'

Yan's deep voice was husky, amused but strained.
'So... you have not been short on moral guidance,
little Lolita?'

'I'm twenty-one, Yan,' she reminded him with a
spark of indignation. 'I'm not little. And I'm not
a Lolita either. I've just... never wanted a man the
way I want you...'

The words were said. The charged pause which
followed emphasised their shattering effect. Yan
very slowly, very carefully turned her face up to

his, kissed her gently on the lips, then swung away to start the engine and drive her back to her lodgings.

'Your colleague will be worried about you,' he pointed out hoarsely, his expression guarded as he waited with what seemed like unflattering impatience for her to get out. '*Kalinichta*, Eleanor.'

'Goodnight...' Was that all? Nothing more? No suggestion they meet tomorrow, no mention of the intimate conversation they'd just shared? Dazed, and unsure of the situation, she stumbled down out of the jeep and walked stiffly into the house. She spent that night in a restless whirl of uncertainty, alternately burning with embarrassment and longing.

Over the next few days Yan was nowhere to be seen. She swallowed her pride sufficiently to go down to the watersports hut the following evening, but he wasn't there. Confused and deeply hurt, she gathered the rags of her pride around her, immersed herself in the infinite variety of her work, and pretended to herself that nothing whatsoever had happened. Nothing important. Just a brief aberration. Just a case of an experienced older man amusing himself at the expense of a gauche younger girl. She'd survive. Once she'd stopped dying of humiliation...

She switched on to auto-pilot, buzzing around on her little moped, doing duty rota at the crowded airport, dealing with complaints, addressing welcome meetings for groups of new tourists, organising boat trips and coach trips and excursions and following Laura's suggestions for social relaxation with a polite lack of enthusiasm which clearly baffled the older girl. Two days later, while she and Laura were having a meal at a small taverna on the hillside above the bay with two of the English male tour representatives, she saw Yan again. He was sitting at a nearby table, with another girl.

He was all in black. Black pleat-waist trousers, loose black silk polo-shirt. His thick black hair was brushed back, the lines of his face severe and autocratic. He looked lean, hard, distant, utterly unobtainable. A total stranger. The girl with him was beautiful: silver top and clinging black leggings, masses of night-dark wavy hair, huge deep-set grey eyes. She was looking at Yan with such yearning intensity that Eleanor felt physically ill. In her pink and white sundress, and simple flat white sandals, she felt like some dowdy schoolgirl compared with this svelte, exotic female holding Yan's attention. Like Milly-Molly-Mandy compared with Cleopatra... So *this* was the reason Yan had swiftly terminated their brief relationship... and how ridiculous she'd been to think a man like Yan Diamakis would ever be interested in Eleanor Carrington, fresh out from England, green as a new shoot, inept, infatuated, pathetic...

Meeting his eyes across the taverna was like receiving an electric shock across the airwaves.

Laura had left the table to go to the loo. The two male tour reps were halfway through their second bottle of retsina and deep in commiseration about their trials with the transfer bus drivers. Desperate to escape, Eleanor fled, white-faced, with the lamest of excuses. Ten minutes later she'd walked up to the main road and was waiting to flag down a taxi to get back to her lodgings when Yan's jeep pulled up beside her, and he hauled her unceremoniously in. She couldn't stop the tears. They stung her eyes, ran down her face.

'Eleanor...' The deep voice was rough with emotion, but forcefully insistent. 'Why did you run from the taverna just now? Why did you walk out and leave your friends?'

'Because I...I...' There was no way she could say the words, complete her humiliation by spelling out the anguish of seeing him with that other girl...

'Don't cry. There is no need to cry. Eleanor, listen! I did not intend to upset you. I had to talk to Sofia...'

'Sofia? Is that her name? So where's poor Sofia now?' She choked angrily, 'Have you just dumped her? The way you dumped me the other night?'

Yan looked a fraction whiter beneath his tan. She wasn't sure, didn't know him well enough to tell, if this was anger, or weariness, or both...

'No. We had finished our meal. And our conversation. Sofia's parents' house is close by. She has returned there.'

'How convenient!'

'You would prefer me to invite you into my bed while I am still involved with another woman?' he queried, softly mocking, but his dark eyes kindling on her flushed, tear-stained cheeks. 'Is that the way men and women behave in your country, Eleanor?'

His words caught her by surprise. The frankness brought a fresh wave of heat to her cheeks—in fact to her whole body. Stomach tightening, she stared at him in confusion, and increasing indignation.

'What makes you think I want to be "invited into your bed?"' she countered, pride giving her voice a stiff coolness which made his lips twitch slightly.

'Don't you, Eleanor?' His voice had thickened slightly, twisting her stomach into knots of fright and longing.

'I...of all the arrogant, conceited...!' She was beside herself with anger. 'How could you make something so...so special sound so...clinical?'

'Something special? How can you be so sure the experience would be special? Beforehand?' The cynical teasing made her seize up inside with embarrassment and humiliation. 'But forgive me,' he mocked hoarsely. 'I was forgetting how very young you are. You would prefer me to veil my suggestion in suitable romantic trimmings.'

Eleanor hardly believed her ears. Was this the man who'd kissed her with such devastating, soul-searching passion on the beach? The man who'd kept her spellbound over dinner that evening in Skiathos?

'What has made you so *cynical*?'

'I am a realist. And at least I am honest, *agapití mou*. In squaring my personal affairs with Sofia, I was taking the honourable course of action. That is the only course open to a man when he meets someone he wants so badly as I want you...'

'So what's the big joke?' she demanded distractedly, seeing that dark laughter in his eyes. 'Is...is this the way you do things in your country?

Everything strictly honourable and...and mocking, and cold-blooded?'

'Cold-blooded? You push me too far...' The re-action was dry, the brilliant glitter in Yan's eyes tinged with angry amusement. With a muted scream of tyres, he pulled away from the roadside and drove at a ferociously controlled speed back to her lodgings.

'I think it is best if we end this right now, before anyone else is hurt,' he said abruptly at the door to the house. He didn't touch her. Her heart seemed to shrink and die inside her. Every nerve screamed to feel his touch, but he kept his distance. 'We are too different, Eleanor. You want perhaps what I cannot give you, little one. So forget it. *Endaxi*? Agreed? *Adio*, Eleanor...'

Choked with dismay, she watched him lope back to his jeep, drive away. In her room she paced the floor, her mind and emotions in shreds. At last, hardly knowing what she was doing, but in the grip of a yearning and a curiosity stronger than any-thing she'd ever known, she walked down to the hotel on the beach, and asked at the reception desk for Yan's private apartment.

With a faint flicker of surprise, the male recep-tionist stared at Eleanor's white, tense face and then kindly directed her to an outer entrance. Three flights of stairs led to a heavy oak door, and when Yan opened it, still damp from a shower, clad only in a small white towel slung perilously low on his hips, she found herself in a spacious penthouse at the top of the hotel. There were shining beech floors and navy and green furnishings. Huge windows showed a panoramic view of the dark expanse of sea. There was a brightly lit ferry visible, framed in the window, plying its way from the mainland to the island.

'Yan, I couldn't sleep; I had to talk to you,' she began shakily, but then stopped at the savage, despairing light in his eyes as he swept a comprehensive gaze over her trembling figure. 'When I said you were cold-blooded, I only meant . . .'

'Yes. I think I know what you meant. But if it is cold-blooded to feel as I do about you,' he grated thickly, catching her by the arm to pull her round fiercely against the warm, muscled wall of his body, 'then fire is cold, Eleanor . . .'

A noise from Christophor, in the room next door, jerked her from her reverie. She shivered convulsively, leaning on the balcony rail. She'd heard those aggressively sensual words again in her head, as if Yan had spoken them right now. What had happened that night to that silly, gullible, over-romantic twenty-one-year-old, and the dreamy, passion-filled weeks that had followed, would stay with her for the rest of her life. But thankfully the searing memories, agonising in their clarity, blurred slightly, and began to fade.

She crept into the bedroom adjoining hers and checked on her son's bed. He was sound asleep. He must have cried out in his sleep. She firmly quelled the urge to lift the warm, sleeping child into her arms and carry him back into her bed, to seek comfort from his warm little body.

However she decided to resolve this mess, one thing was clear. Christophor was the most important person to consider. He was not to be dragged into the emotional turmoil any more than could be helped. Everything must stay as calm and normal as possible...

Going back into her room, she slid into bed and lay on her back, beneath the starched white sheet. She was still so furious with Yan that the anger and resentment fizzed through her veins. She had to think, but somehow it was so hard to think. There were so many things she had to think about. Nothing was straightforward. Nothing was as she'd expected it to be. The only constant was Christophor, her love for her little son. The past was not his fault. It was unthinkable that Christophor should suffer because of her past mistakes. Or her present ones...

But...*marry* Yan? The man's arrogance took her breath away. She clenched her hands at her sides, just thinking about his nonchalant pronouncement. Marriage between them was unthinkable. She'd been humiliated enough at his hands four years ago. There was no way she would swallow her pride this time...

There had to be a solution, she reflected exhaustedly. Some way of jolting Yan Diamakis into the twentieth century...

When she became aware of the brilliance of the morning sun through her window, she realised she must have slept. She jumped out of bed, and found her watch. She hadn't just slept, she'd *overslept*.

Darting next door, she found Christophor's bed empty. Sounds of voices drifted up from the terrace below. Childish laughter, the deep tone of Yan's

voice. Trembling with impatience, Eleanor showered and dressed, hesitated at the pine cheval mirror
just long enough to brush the heavy curtain of
brown hair into obedience and check the neatness
of white shorts and loose navy silk over-blouse.
Thrusting her bare feet into strappy leather sandals,
she ran downstairs in the direction of the voices.

At the entrance to the terrace, beside a dense
curtain of purple bougainvillaea and green vine
leaves, she stopped abruptly. The group on the
terrace, lingering over breakfast at a long, white-
clothed table with starched napkins and silver coffee
service, included Yan sipping coffee, Christophor
busily devouring a hard-boiled egg with a slice of
cheese, Evangelie hovering to top up the coffee-
cups, and a woman whose cloudy dark hair and
huge, intense grey eyes triggered instant recognition.

The pain which shot through her was so powerful
that Eleanor needed to grip on to the wall to support
herself. Sofia. Of course. Of course, Yan should
have married Sofia. And even if he was still offering marriage to Eleanor, because of their son, it
appeared that he and Sofia were still very much
together...

As she stepped forward, heart thudding, throat
tight, Sofia glanced up and saw her. Her lips moved
as she said something to Yan, who turned around,
his dark face deadpan as he watched her approach.

'Mummy!' At least Christophor seemed unaf-
fectedly pleased to see her, she thought bleakly,
gathering her son in her arms as he raced around
the table to greet her.

'*Kalimera*, Eleanor. How nice to see you again.' Sofia's greeting couldn't have been less sincere. Strolling to join them at the table, Eleanor hid her feelings behind a bland, unconcerned smile, nearly as impassive as Yan's expression. But inside she felt a squeeze of cold fear in her heart. Were Yan and Sofia playing at happy families, perhaps? Imagining Christophor as *their* son?

The squeeze of fear was followed by such an acute wave of fury that she had to clench her teeth to suppress it.

'Aunty Sofia said she and Papa would take me on the boat today!' Christophor was saying excitedly.

'*Really*?' Eleanor steeled herself. Wanting only what was best for Christophor was one thing. Meekly allowing herself to be blackmailed into handing him over to Yan and Sofia was another. 'Well, I think your daddy has forgotten that he is far too busy running his hotel today, sweetheart. And Aunty Sofia has probably forgotten that she has a...a hair appointment. So how about you and me going *riding* instead?'

The frown that had briefly touched the small forehead was quickly ironed out.

'Horse-riding!' Thumb in mouth, Christophor nodded vigorous approval.

'That's settled, then. Thanks for the kind thought—some other time, maybe?' Eleanor flashed a cool smile, skimming over the glitter of ice in Sofia's eyes and flicking determinedly over the wary amusement in Yan's. Sofia said something in Greek to Yan, and he replied. As always with the Greek language and intonation, Eleanor found it was hard to tell if the exchange was pleasant or acrimonious.

As she sat down to choose French bread, hard-boiled egg and coffee for her breakfast, she was acutely aware of Yan's nearness. Cool and relaxed in denims and loose forest-green shirt, long legs stretched out casually in front of him, it was impossible to tell what he was thinking.

'Are you in the mood for riding this morning, Sofia?' he queried with a wry quirk of his lips.

'No. I think not. Besides, I have just remembered, I have to go into Skiathos Town and attend to some business in the boutique...' Abruptly the other girl stood up, smoothing down flame-coloured culottes and white, cowl-neck silk blouse with a quick, annoyed movement.

'Pity. Some other time, then?' Yan too stood up, impeccably courteous.

'*Endaxi. Adio...*' There was a kiss for Christophor, and a cool, challenging glance for Eleanor, before Sofia walked quickly off the terrace and disappeared.

'That was not very polite.' Yan's tone was conversational.

Eleanor, watching her son dangling a piece of cheese for a lean tabby cat who'd been sunning itself by the wall, gave a tense shrug.

'Don't make arrangements for my child without consulting me,' she snapped, unable to stop herself.

'*Our* child,' Yan reminded her calmly. 'Is he old enough to ride safely?'

'Of course. There is a stables next to the hotel in Northumberland. Christophor learned to ride almost before he could walk...'

'Here you will have to make do with mules.' Yan grinned, folding his arms as he sat down again beside her. 'But I agree. Riding sounds a very pleasant way of spending the morning. I'll drive us up to the riding school in, let me see, half an hour's time?'

'You don't need to come...'

'But I wish to.' There was an inflexible note in Yan's deep voice. 'And it will give us an opportunity to talk.'

'Apart from agreeing on some kind of access arrangements for Christophor, I don't think we have a lot to talk about...'

'On the contrary. I confess to a burning curiosity.'

'Oh?' Her throat felt dryer suddenly. 'About what?'

'About why you broke our engagement four years ago. Why you lied to me about the baby you were carrying. And why you wrote to me, confessing the truth, after all this time.'

Yan stood up again, his eyes unreadable. 'And then, of course, there is the question of our forthcoming marriage, *ne*? I think those interesting questions should ensure that we have enough to talk about, Eleanor. Don't you agree?'

Lifting her chin defiantly, she met his eyes with a level gaze.

'There isn't a forthcoming marriage, Yan,' she said flatly, steeling herself to stand up to him. 'At least, not between you and me. Because I'm afraid that . . . I'm planning to marry someone else!'

CHAPTER THREE

THE words had just tumbled out, the most dramatic line of defence that sprang to mind. Now, though, facing the ominous tautening of Yan's dark face, Eleanor cursed her impulsiveness. Lowering her eyes, she took time over pouring herself more coffee. She could feel Yan's narrowed gaze on her, almost like a physical assault.

'Is this true, Eleanor?' The deep voice held a grim note, but it was hard to gauge his precise feelings. Yan was skilled at hiding his real feelings, she reflected bleakly. She'd learned that the hard way, hadn't she?

'Would I lie to you?' Her choice of flippancy was unfortunate. She bit her lip as he gave a short, hard laugh.

'Oh, yes, indeed.' His drawl was bitterly sardonic.

She had the grace to colour slightly. Damn the man. How did he manage to make her feel permanently in the wrong, after his abominable . . . no, criminal behaviour in snatching Christophor from his home in England?

'And I suppose you've never lied to me?' she countered, glancing over at her small son, who had hopped down from the table during this boring adult conversation, and was now virtually force-feeding the cat with the remains of his breakfast.

'About what?'

'That's right, answer a question with a question—the classic evasion . . .'

'What have I lied to you about, Eleanor?'

'About *Sofia*?' It almost choked her to say the girl's name, she realised with a jolt of dismay. Surely she couldn't still feel even the remotest twinge of jealousy about whoever Yan chose to spend his time with?

'I do not recall lying to you about Sofia.' Yan's cool tone revealed no emotion. He seemed to have retreated behind some invisible guard, watchful, ominously patient.

'So what do you call that proposal of marriage to me, four years ago? That was the biggest lie I ever came across!'

'I proposed marriage four years ago because I wanted to marry you, Eleanor.' Yan regarded her steadily for what seemed an endless time. When she could bear the mounting tension no longer she stood up abruptly, abandoning her breakfast, and went to arbitrate between Christophor and the unfortunate cat.

'No, sweetheart,' she remonstrated gently, picking up her son and giving him a hug. 'The cat's had enough cheese. I don't think cheese is his favourite food . . .'

'What does the cat want to eat?' Christophor wanted to know, grabbing her blouse in fingers that were decidedly sticky. Yan came to stand beside them, his dark gaze amused.

'Mice, frogs and birds,' he said with solemn attention to realism, 'if he's fast enough to catch them.' He reached to ruffle the child's dark hair, with a gesture so natural and loving that Eleanor felt her heart squeeze painfully in her chest. 'Wash your hands, little one. Then your mummy and I will take you riding. *Endaxi*?'

''*Daxi*,' agreed Christophor gravely, amazing his mother with his rapid grasp of the foreign language.

'I'd have thought you'd far rather be spending the morning sailing with Sofia,' she said to Yan half an hour later as they rode, side-saddle Greek-style, along the thickly wooded ridge above the bay. The sea looked like shimmering blue satin far below, framed in fronds of cypress and juniper. Christophor, perched precariously on his large mule, looked ridiculously small but extremely important. Yan had him on a leading-rein. There was a pervasive air of a little family unit about the outing. It made her nervous, edgier than ever. She couldn't just relax into this parody of domesticity with Yan Diamakis...

'Then you would have been wrong, Eleanor. I am much more interested in spending the morning with my son, his mother, and hearing all about this *fiancé* back in England.'

She glanced at him, angry and perplexed by his unruffled air of containment. Whatever was going on in his mind, or in his heart, he was guarding it all behind a mask of bland composure. It made her feel far more uneasy than a blatant display of hostility or aggression...

'Yan,' she began at last, 'I realise you're angry about...the past. About my not telling you that Christophor was born...'

'You make it sound like an absent-minded omission,' he cut in acidly, 'when, in fact, it was a deliberate, premeditated deception. When, in fact, you lied, in that cowardly little note you left for me, about not being pregnant.'

'You must understand my reasons . . .' she began, her throat drying.

'No. I will never understand your reasons, Eleanor.'

'Well, I don't think I'll ever understand your motives in all this . . .' she retorted in a low, angry voice.

'In all what?'

'Stealing Christophor. Luring me out here like this . . .'

Hesitating, she found herself caught up in the dark intensity of his gaze. 'Pretending you want to spend time with me. Unless it's revenge, of course . . .'

'You make me sound a petty-minded tyrant.'

'You said it.'

'I had hoped that by now you would have grown up.' Yan's voice was coolly derisive. 'Your recent letter was . . .' he laughed shortly ' . . . unexpected? That would be the ironic English understatement, *ne*? But when I had controlled my first furious reaction I read your letter again, and I thought you might have matured. It seems I was wrong.'

Heat was creeping into her face.

'I have matured. It's a measure of your own *immaturity* that you can doubt it,' she said stiffly. 'Having a child is the quickest route to growing up,

Yan. Bringing him up alone accelerates things even more.'

The dark eyes were unreadable as he glanced across at her.

'You did not have to bring him up alone. That was your choice. And you say you are mature, but your actions belie your words.'

'What gives you the right to sit there and . . . and *judge* my character . . . ?'

'I was your first lover,' he said coolly, his casual words sending hot shafts of agonised sensation deep into her stomach. 'Do you remember? You were *parthénos*, virgin, that night you came to my apartment and we made love, Eleanor. And the next two months we were together for as many hours as we could be. I thought I knew you. I think your subsequent behaviour towards me gives me the right to judge your character.'

His iron control was goading her unbearably. His voice was low enough to be inaudible to a three-year-old engrossed in strange sights and sounds around him. From his tone he could be discussing the view framed through the clearing in the pine wood, commenting on the radiant sea and sun-drenched, mystical hillsides surrounding them.

How could he ask if she remembered? That night was deeply etched in her subconscious. Yan's impact on her life had been like a powerful tidal wave, swamping every other consideration . . .

He went on quietly, 'Now you write to tell me that I have a son. That what I believed to have happened four years ago did not happen. That you did not tragically miscarry our baby and cancel our engagement for that reason. That you deliberately lied, and ran away to England, bore my son without my knowledge...'

'Yan——'

'You give me your address, therefore inviting my visit. But when I present myself on your doorstep, Eleanor, you are cold and unwelcoming...'

'What did you expect? That I'd be waiting in a see-through négligé...?' The bitter fury in her voice went unremarked.

'And you refuse permission for my son to visit his homeland...'

'And so you thought that gave you the right to snatch him back to Greece, leaving me a... high-handed, arrogant note and an air ticket?'

'Did you not leave me a note four years ago, before vanishing with my unborn child?' Yan's voice was implacable. 'At least I had the generosity of spirit to tell you where to find us.'

'An eye for an eye? I might have known! England is his homeland,' she whispered angrily. 'For heaven's sake stop behaving like some... some xenophobic autocrat!'

'Make some effort to see things from my point of view, Eleanor. Our child was conceived here in Greece,' Yan continued conversationally, unperturbed by her trembling outburst.

'But you are only half Greek,' she countered with increasing obstinacy. 'Your mother was English. I am English. *That* makes Christophor more English than Greek, so...'

Yan shrugged, a faint twitch of humour on his mouth, but there was that hard gleam in his eyes which made her only too aware of the pointlessness of her arguments. There'd always been that inflexible, autocratic core to Yan. It had attracted her but frightened her at the same time. It could make her feel secure, and safe and protected. But also it made her feel very young and inept and vulnerable. That had been only one of the many reasons for acting as she had, but it had been an emotive one. If she'd been assured of Yan's love, these reservations would have been too flimsy to matter. Nothing would have mattered. She would have consented to anything, even to a lifetime's servitude, if she'd known beyond any doubt that Yan loved her as much as she loved him...

But Yan's love had never been assured. It had always been in doubt. Even after that cataclysmic initiation into the rites of physical passion, that night in his hotel apartment...

Memories swirling uncontrollably in her head, her stomach churning with nerves, she realised that she'd been too distracted to listen to what Yan was saying.

'Shall we go back?' he murmured, nodding at Christophor's fidgeting air of boredom. 'In Greece, the siesta still rules the day. For adults as well as three-year-olds...'

There was something in the narrowed, faintly amused dark gaze that made her catch her breath involuntarily. Thoughts of that first time together, of Yan's fiercely tender assault on her senses, had been scorching a destructive path through her thoughts. Had he somehow tuned in? She shuddered at the idea.

'You talk of seeing things from your point of view,' she said quickly, to cover her fear and embarrassment, as they swung the mules around and headed back through the woods, 'but what about the other way round? You're so...so blinkered, you can't even begin to see that a mere *woman* might have a mind of her own, a life of her own, a free *choice* in...in pregnancy and birth and motherhood and a career...'

'You're wrong, Eleanor. I can see all that,' he retorted coolly. 'But you are forgetting the child. If you believe it is best for Christophor to be brought up without his real father, perhaps believing that his father does not want him, you are wrong. A boy needs a father. I am that father. You presumably accept this fact, or you would not have written to me.'

There was a sick lump in her throat. Yan's words, unwelcome, didactic though they might be, couldn't fail to strike home. Whatever the emotions that had driven her to act the way she had four years ago, or the emotions that had compelled her to tell him the truth now, the cold facts, set out in this logical way, made unpleasant listening.

'Biologically, yes, I accept that you're his father...'

There was a chilling silence following this statement.

'But now you are calmly telling me that there is another man in England who wants to fill this role. Who is this man? What is his name? What does he do for a living?'

The trace of steel in the deep voice sent a shiver down her spine.

'He's a homeopathic doctor. His name is... is Geoffrey. Geoffrey Terence-Evans...'

'Do you think I will stand by and watch my son grow up with a quack doctor called Geoffrey Terence-Evans as his father?' The explosion of black derision in Yan's voice made her clench her teeth.

A sense of panic was driving her pulse-rate sky-high.

'Geoffrey is *not* a quack doctor! Don't be ridiculous! And if... if relationships break up, often one partner has to stand by and watch their child grow up with a... a step-parent. You can't *force* your overbearing ideas on people...'

Their bitter, low-voiced exchange came to an end. They were back at the riding school, handing over their mounts. Christophor looked flushed and tired as she lifted him down and hugged him.

'Maybe the siesta isn't such a bad thing for you, young man.' She smiled as he clasped hot hands round her neck and caught a thick lock of nut-brown hair to hold while the inevitable thumb went into his mouth. 'How about an early lunch, a little sleep and then a play on the beach?'

The suggestion met with approval. Evangelie was waiting, tempting menu ready to coax a small child's appetite, keen to fulfil her role as Christophor's devoted slave, when they got back to the house.

'He'll be spoiled rotten by all this attention,' she pointed out, watching her son's small retreating back as he was led off to his bedroom for his afternoon nap after a robust meal of grilled sole, boiled potatoes and rich Greek yogurt and honey. She found herself alone with Yan again, drinking coffee on the shady terrace, her eyes carefully fixed on the view of the bay, with the icing-sugar-white launch bobbing at anchor in the midday sun.

'Then that is a strong argument for getting things on a normal footing.'

'I fully intend to. When I take him back home to England——'

'I notice you gave him a Greek name. Christophoros.' Yan's cool interruption, ignoring the provocation of her words, took her by surprise.

'Half Greek. I left off the last two letters. Compromised. English schoolchildren can be cruel about anything too unusual . . .'

'Why? If you hated Greece, and me, and everything I stood for, why give your baby a Greek name?'

Yan had leaned back in his chair, hands thrust in the pockets of his jeans, legs sprawled in front of him. He was watching her with that intent gaze which never failed to unnerve her.

Reaching a shaky hand behind her neck to lift the weight of her hair from her nape, she felt his eyes move to the swell of her breasts beneath the navy silk blouse. His mood was enigmatic, but she felt terribly vulnerable. After his cuttingly hostile mockery over Geoffrey, there was something ominous about his renewed air of patient investigation.

'I didn't hate Greece—how could I? I love it . . .'

'Then it was just me that you hated,' he agreed impassively, registering no emotion. 'Why, Eleanor? Why did you fool me into thinking you loved me?'

'Love and hate are two sides of the same coin, aren't they?' She kept her voice similarly cool. Anything to keep the volcanic emotions from erupting to the surface, blowing her cover wide open. 'And I...I didn't hate you, Yan. I was just...afraid...'

Terrified of how much I loved you, she wanted to say. But that would be fatal. To give him the smallest leverage into trapping her again...

'You must have hated me very much to have lied the way you did, Eleanor. And yet I could have staked my life on the fact that you loved me.'

'I was infatuated. It's not the same. It doesn't last...'

'You say you were afraid. Of what? Of me?'

When she couldn't find the words to answer him, he mused slowly, 'To be afraid of someone implies they have some kind of power over you...' He turned to inspect her flushed cheeks with a steady, lidded appraisal. 'Are you afraid of me now, Eleanor?'

The deep voice was a fraction huskier. It touched a chord inside her. Pain shot through her like a physical knife-wound.

Moistening her lips involuntarily, she shook her head with a quick, negative movement.

'I'm not afraid of you. The only thing I'm afraid of is of someone hurting Christophor. Whoever did that, I think I would kill them...'

'So savage and protective.'

He took a calm swig of his coffee, slanting a sardonic eyebrow at her white, tense face. 'And this homeopath called Geoffrey...' The sneer in his voice intensified. 'How long have you known him?'

'I...I met him on a course in aromatherapy. Just before Christophor was born...'

'Aromatherapy?'

'Massage with essential oils. It's an alternative medicine...'

'Yes. I do know what it is. I wondered why you had chosen to do a course in it, that's all.'

'I thought it might be a useful addition to the health and beauty facilities at my aunt's hotel...'

'Do you live with him?' Yan cut in abruptly.

'No...' The proverbial tangled web, she thought as she evaded Yan's penetrating gaze. Her heart had begun to thud against her ribcage as if it might burst. Her palms felt moist.

'Are you sleeping with him?'

'That's none of your damned business!'

'You're not wearing an engagement ring,' Yan pointed out implacably, his narrowed gaze watching the colour surge and recede in her face with what appeared to be detached speculation.

'No. Not yet, but the engagement is semi-official...'

'Write him a letter,' Yan suggested indifferently. 'Tell him you are marrying the father of your child.'

'You're crazy!' It was difficult to tell if Yan was cruelly teasing or totally serious. 'It would never work,' she went on, as calmly as she could. 'You didn't love me four years ago, Yan...'

'So I recall you telling me at the time...'

'And you don't love me now...!'

They were silent for a while, bitter pride and confusion lacerating the tension between them.

'Love,' he said at last, his voice bleak, 'doesn't come into it.' He turned the full brilliance of his gaze on her, like a dark laser beam. 'Nor does trust,' he added cuttingly. 'Do you imagine I could trust you? After what you did to me?'

'After what *I* did to *you*?' she managed to choke. Her pretence at calm was over. She gazed at him through a blur of tears, fiercely suppressed. 'You were the one who offered marriage out of *pity*! And some stupid, misguided sense of honour and duty. Just because you found out I was pregnant. You were the one who...who pretended you were heart-free, when all the time you were engaged to marry your second cousin Sofia! You *used* me, Yan. All that summer. It was just a game to you. A game of conquest. A game to gratify your *ego*...'

'A virgin sacrifice to Apollo the sun-god?' he suggested, bitter irony in his voice.

'I've rather lost interest in Greek mythology,' she countered stiffly, 'but I suppose you'll never stop throwing that *immature* fascination in my face, will you? As for your suggestions, Yan, frankly they *stink*! A marriage with no trust?' she finished scornfully, getting unsteadily to her feet. 'With no love? We'd despise each other within a few months! Do you think *that* environment is the best for our child?'

Yan stood up too, taking firm hold of her upper arm before she could stalk off the terrace to escape.

'Calm yourself,' he said, a gentler note in his voice which flayed her even more than the previous icy censure or searing mockery. 'Come, Eleanor. I apologise if I have deeply offended you. We'll have lunch over at the hotel, and see if we cannot arrive at some ... compromise?'

'I can't leave Christophor...'

'Evangelie will watch Christophor like a mother hawk. He trusts her, and you have seen how she adores him.'

This was patently true. After a short, silent struggle with her emotions, she shrugged and nodded jerkily. No matter how bitter the atmosphere between herself and Yan, there wasn't much gain in stalking off to brood in silence.

As they walked the short distance to the hotel, she mulled over Yan's use of the word 'compromise'. Compromise? Why did the word lack any ring of conviction? she wondered frustratedly. Because she doubted if the word genuinely formed part of Yan's vocabulary? The unfathomable light in his eyes did nothing to allay her suspicions.

The beach bar at the hotel was cool and spacious, shaded by a huge pergola of vines, fanned by the sea breeze, and surrounded by flowers: velvety purple petunias, geraniums in all shades of pink and red, scented yellow and white roses, and richly perfumed honeysuckle. It was a setting designed to relax and appeal to the senses of the hotel's guests. And as a place to have lunch, it was very hard to beat, Eleanor had to admit, reflecting on the chilly east wind which howled around Aunt Meg's hotel.

The waiters this year were, as before, smiling, polite, good-natured. Seated at the white-clothed table, with the sea just a few yards away, Eleanor chose a Greek salad, with its refreshing mix of feta cheese, olives, tomatoes and peppers, accepted a glass of cool white wine, and tried, very hard, to relax a little.

In fact, she realised belatedly, relaxing wasn't as impossible as it seemed. Yan could exercise considerable skill as a conversationalist when the occasion suited him. And in the congenial surroundings, with the light-hearted presence of holiday-makers enjoying their annual fortnight in the sun, it was dangerously easy to relax a little too much. Providing the fatally provocative subjects of her pregnancy, Christophor and marriage were put into temporary abeyance, the last four years might hardly have intervened in the subtle but unnervingly strong rapport she shared with Yan Diamakis.

Service, as always seemed the case in Greece, was on a laid-back, leisurely time-scale. While they waited for their food, Eleanor found they were discussing Yan's father's retirement to a house up in the hills, the burgeoning shipping and airline industry, the cost of living in London and Athens, the hotel business, and comparing Aunt Meg's hotel with the Thessa Beach. She could be catching up on news with an old friend, she reflected with a slight jolt. There was a lull in their conversation. Was Yan thinking what she'd been thinking—how deceptively easily they'd slipped back into a warm

air of companionship? Or was this cleverly or-
chestrated? Was Yan determinedly and cleverly
manipulating her into a more receptive frame of
mind?

She pushed her wine glass cautiously away, and
poured herself some mineral water.

'Do you still water-ski?' The question was casual.
She glanced up at Yan and found the hard lines of
his face unreadable, as usual.

'Hardly. I don't have the time or the weather
conditions where I live.'

'You were a star pupil,' he recalled with a faint
smile in his eyes. 'By the end of that summer you
were nearly as good as me.'

'Such modesty!'

'Of course. It doesn't pay to become conceited.'

She had to smile at the twist of self-mockery in
his expression.

'There's always someone around to knock you
back down to size if you get too sure of yourself,'
he added obliquely as her salad and his grilled sole
arrived.

'So tell me about your hotel's health and fitness
clinic,' he went on. 'You say you are in charge of
the leisure facilities?' Was he relentlessly steering
the conversation away from danger areas? To lull
her into a false security?

'Yes. In fact it was my idea. My aunt has let me
build up the whole thing from scratch. We don't
exactly rival the top health farms, but we come
pretty close...' In spite of her resolution, she found
herself sipping some more wine to steady her nerves.

'It's doing very well. Things like the aromatherapy service are really popular...'

'Do you do the massage personally?' The slightest quirk of his eyebrow alerted her to an underlying amusement. Or was it disapproval?

'Some of it, yes. But there is a full-time beauty therapist we employ as well. We see guests for a full consultation, to decide which oil combination would be right for that person's needs. We do a whole-body massage, with essential aromatic oils.' She cleared her throat at the gleam in the narrowed dark eyes across the table. 'It's becoming very popular in England. And it's very therapeutic. It can actually *cure* some chronic illnesses.'

'And are your regular clients male or female?'

She levelled a straight look at him.

'Female. Purely coincidental, I assure you. Women tend to be more aware of the benefits of alternative medicine...'

'So if a male guest asked you for a full-body massage, you'd be happy to oblige?'

'Of course. Why not?' Her temper flared at that cynical glint in his eye. 'I'm not running a...a sleazy *massage parlour*, for heaven's sake! There's nothing *sexual* about aromatherapy massage, Yan!'

He was grinning at her furious reaction, but she was too annoyed to see the joke.

'Can't men ever separate their *basic* instincts from a more...spiritual level?' she bit out, then stopped as he burst out laughing.

'You haven't changed at all,' he told her, with a mocking shake of his head. 'Still a little romantic, head in the clouds, seeing the world through innocent eyes.'

'Don't patronise me, Yan. I'm twenty-five, a single parent, and I have a successful career. It's your vision that's faulty. Not mine!'

'You sound very sure of yourself, Eleanor. Very single-minded. Perhaps that, too, shows you haven't changed.'

Yan was non-committal. Infuriatingly ambiguous.

She was about to retort when Sofia appeared, cool-eyed and smiling, beside their table. She bent to speak to Yan in rapid, incomprehensible Greek, one manicured hand on his shoulder. A waft of expensive perfume floated Eleanor's way.

Glancing at his watch, Yan glanced coolly across the table.

'Forgive me, Eleanor. I have some things to attend to here at the hotel this afternoon. One of our receptionists has been taken ill. There are various crises looming, so I am informed.'

He grinned as he stood up, adding casually, 'No doubt you'll find enough to keep yourself amused until this evening.'

Incredulously she stared at him, fighting the reprehensible urge to throw something at the smugly triumphant Sofia hovering behind him. His mockery over her aromatherapy skills had fuelled her anger all over again. And his supercilious opinion of her as some naïve, starry-eyed innocent was utterly infuriating. But for some reason it was this casual dismissal that was hurting her pride most fiercely of all.

What was wrong with her? She didn't want the hateful man's company, did she? The longer he spent attending to business, the less she'd be subjected to his domineering presence! And since she'd long ago imagined him firmly married to Sofia, surely, *surely* she wasn't jealous at seeing him so easily lured away from their lunch together?

'I'm quite *sure* I shall keep myself "amused", as you so charmingly put it! A few telephone calls to England for starters...'

'Ah, yes. To *Geoffrey*, perhaps?'

'That's none of your damn business, Yan! And anyway, just how long is this...*charade* going on for?' she demanded huskily. 'I've got a job to do back in England, as you know! Do you imagine I'm here in Skiathos, at your beck and call, indefinitely? Or am I a prisoner, perhaps?'

'A prisoner?' he mused, deadpan. 'Do not overdramatise the situation. But which is more important? Your job in England, or our son's future? You must see that we have important matters to sort out.'

She bit her lip, speechless at this emotional blackmail. He had a point, she knew he did. Christophor's future was the single most important issue here. They did have a problem, which had to be sorted out one way or another. It was just his *arrogant*, high-handed method of approaching it which left a great deal to be desired.

'Relax,' he advised, softly patronising. 'You look pale and tense, Eleanor. Swim, sunbathe, water-ski. Evangelie will look after Christophor. *Adio*. I will see you later.'

To her muted fury, he bent casually to kiss her full on the lips. What felt like a thousand volts of painful awareness rocketed through her veins.

Watching him saunter calmly into the hotel, dark head bent to listen to whatever Sofia was saying to him, she hardly dared to analyse the dark thoughts swirling round in her head.

CHAPTER FOUR

So, AS well as that little ceramics boutique her family owned in Skiathos Town, Sofia now worked in the hotel, with Yan? It wasn't so strange, now she thought about it. The Diamakis family were fairly close-knit, as she bitterly recalled. Sofia was Aunt Maria's stepdaughter. Aunt Maria was Yan's father's sister, who'd married a widower. So the cousin relationship was tenuous in theory but fairly strong in practice. Nearly as strong as the family's determination to see the stepcousins marry and presumably forge a solid new generation for the Diamakis family business empire . . .

What had happened, then, to that much desired marriage? Who was holding fire? Yan or Sofia? Surely not Sofia, after what she'd said to Eleanor four years ago. Then it must have been Yan. Yan who'd delayed the marriage . . .

A small, stubborn flicker of hope leaped into tentative life in Eleanor's heart as she walked slowly back around the headland to the house. Had she . . . was there some way that she'd misread the truth, four years ago? Was it possible that she'd got it all wrong?

Common sense briskly doused the small flame of optimism. Agonising over whether she'd made the right decision four years ago was self-destructive. Yan might never have had any more intention of marrying Sofia than of marrying Eleanor. He'd deceived her over his true relationship with the Greek girl. Didn't that show that he was a basic philanderer who took no relationship particularly seriously? Now he was probably giving Sofia the runaround as well. That didn't really change anything. It just proved that the only commitment of true importance to Yan Diamakis was the existence of his *child*.

Eleanor jumped down off the last rock, on to the soft sand of Yan's private beach, and felt a tight little twist of pride and fear in her stomach. There he was, her little son, but also *Yan's* son. Ironically, a tiny replica of the man she'd loved so much ...

She stopped, watching the scene with mixed emotions.

Christophor was on the beach, in the shade of a big sun-umbrella, playing contentedly with two slightly older children, a girl and a boy. A niece and nephew of Evangelie's. The housekeeper had mentioned their visit earlier. Ideal little playmates for Christophor. The three dark heads were bent intently on something they were examining in the sand. Evangelie was supervising from a chair on the terrace. It all looked so happy, so idyllic ... Christophor looked so at home ... Strengthening her resolve, she walked quickly up the beach to meet them.

'Hello, darling!' Christophor had seen her, come running halfway to meet her. She swept the warm, sturdy little body up into her arms, and hugged and kissed him with a fierce surge of bittersweet emotion. Maybe Yan's callousness wouldn't have hurt so much if she hadn't *loved* him so much ... if she hadn't expected so much of their love ...

Christophor was chuckling as she blew a playful raspberry against his neck, held him up in the air as she smiled at him. He was happy, healthy, well-balanced. She'd given him all the love in the world, hadn't she? Everything a child needed. Except a father. But if she'd stayed here and meekly married Yan because of her pregnancy, she'd have transformed herself into a doormat. She wasn't the doormat type. He'd done the honourable thing in proposing marriage, but in reality Yan probably wouldn't have cared *which* female bore him a child. The only fact that mattered was that the baby had been conceived, that the child was his ...

Where was the love, the respect, the partnership, when a man took that view of life? Where did that leave her?

And when he tired of her and took up with other women, perhaps even walked out on her the way her father had on her mother? How could she ever handle such anguish? She never wanted to put herself into a position where she might have to ...

She was sitting in one of the cane chairs, the words of a detective story dancing meaninglessly beneath her eyes, her thoughts far away and singularly unpleasant, when Evangelie ushered Sofia on to the terrace.

'Don't get up,' advised the Greek girl, with one of her coolest smiles, sitting down in the wicker chair next to Eleanor's. She'd changed from this morning's red culottes and top, and now wore a silky leopard-print overshirt and tight white leggings. With her dark curls piled high on her head, and the glimmer of gold jewellery, she exuded such overpoweringly feline sexuality that Eleanor felt like moving to another chair. 'Yan's still tied up at the hotel. There are all sorts of crises looming over staff shortages. But I thought I'd come and say hello properly. We didn't have a chance this morning, did we? What a surprise you gave us all.'

The husky voice, more thickly accented than Yan's, was bland, polite enough, but somehow loaded with innuendo. Her sweeping appraisal of Eleanor's appearance suggested that she found the white shorts and loose navy blouse unutterably provincial and dowdy.

Seeing her again at such close quarters, Eleanor felt her stomach sink. Sofia Theopolou was so…delectably beautiful. With her willowy curves, and full, luscious breasts, bra-less beneath the leopard-print top, and those heavy-lidded eyes, it was easy to see how no man could possibly resist her. The only mystery in the equation was that Yan hadn't married her in the intervening four years. Obviously they were still close, or Sofia wouldn't have been having breakfast with them this very morning…

Evangelie appeared with a tray of tea and some small cakes. Politely Eleanor poured the strong brew, black with lemon for Sofia, and passed one of the blue and gold ceramic cups with a slightly shaking hand across the small round cane table.

'You said I gave you all a surprise?' she queried warily. 'In what way?'

'Why, your letter to Yan. Presenting him with a son, after leaving that note telling everyone you weren't pregnant after all.'

She came straight to the point, Eleanor reflected wryly, levelling a steady gaze at the other girl. And the phrase 'telling everyone' was ironically accurate. She'd left the note to Yan, and no one else. But in the Diamakis family, there appeared to be no loyalty and no secrets...

'Why did you do it?' Sofia persisted softly. The glitter of malice in her eyes was unmistakable.

'That's personal, between Yan and myself,' Eleanor replied shortly. She glanced down the beach. The children were running in and out of the sea with shrieks of enjoyment. Christophor was flapping his orange water-wings up and down, pretending to be Batman.

Sofia followed her gaze, then smiled slightly. A pitying sort of smile, Eleanor decided bleakly.

'Christophor is beautiful, isn't he? He adores Yan. And they are so alike, are they not?'

'There is a definite resemblance,' she agreed, with a passable attempt at calm humour. 'Are you fond of children?'

'I adore them.' Sofia smoothed her thick, curly fringe off her forehead, flashing gold rings on nearly all her fingers. 'I very much hope to have some of my own, one day soon. Yan and I have talked about it a lot...'

'That's nice.' As the Greek girl's words sank home, Eleanor felt almost physically ill, a heavy ache cramping her insides.

'It's pathetic, you know,' the other girl said softly, following up the barb with the killer thrust, 'flinging yourself at Yan all over again. Using Christophor as leverage...'

'Sofia...' It took great self-control not to jump to her feet and run into the house. Summoning all her reserves of poise, Eleanor turned to face the other girl. 'As far as I'm concerned, you and Yan can have as many children as you like. You can both get married tomorrow, and start a population explosion together, for all I care! All I wanted was for Christophor to *know* who his father is, to know that his father cares about him!'

'Of course Yan cares about him!' The Greek girl's face had whitened slightly at Eleanor's reference to marriage. Her full mouth had tightened. 'What Greek man does not care passionately about his son? Why do you think he brought him back here to Skiathos? Because he was concerned about his welfare in England, with you! And it's just as well you prefer your independence and your hotel work to caring for Yan's child. At least you will not miss him so much when you return to England without him!'

There was a crash. Looking down in horror, Eleanor realised that the blue and gold cup had slipped from her nerveless fingers and smashed into small pieces on the terracotta tiles of the patio. The girl's vitriolic words seemed to lash around her, like invisible whiplashes, in the shocked vacuum of silence which followed.

'What makes you think I'd dream of returning to England without *my* son?' she whispered at last.

'You heard. Do you think Yan would let him go back with *you*?'

'I think,' Eleanor said slowly, lifting her chin and steadying a grim sea-green gaze on Sofia, 'that you'd be well advised to keep your nose out of other people's business.'

'If you're fondly imagining yourself married to Yan, think again!' Sofia advised pityingly. 'In Greece marriage is very different from in England, I think. Here in Skiathos, wives are for doing the housework, having babies! You are not even allowed out without your husband, unless you are with a member of the family! You would not last five minutes if you married Yan...'

'Is that why you've put it off so long?' Eleanor stood up, trembling all over, just as Evangelie came out and with a slight shake of her head began picking up the broken shards of blue and gold china. 'Don't worry, Evangelie. I'll clean that up... I think you'd better go, Sofia.'

With an unrepentant smile, the girl swung on her heel and strolled to the door.

'I'm going. But don't forget what I said. You are out of your depth with Yan Diamakis. Think about it, Eleanor. *Adio*.'

It was time for Christophor's afternoon nap. With Evangelie more than happy to be in charge of the procedure, and Christophor content to go with her, Eleanor found herself alone again, with Sofia's words ringing in her head, hard and taunting. She knew she should cool down, swim, relax a little, try to think straight. But she felt so agitated that all she could think of was to tackle

Yan outright, demand to know whether Sofia was telling the truth. Would he still be at the hotel?

Suddenly it seemed the most urgent thing in the world to see him, extract his true intentions, force a show-down...

In the intense heat of mid-afternoon, she almost ran the distance to the hotel.

'Yan, I have to talk to you...!'

'I am listening.' The cool response was accompanied by a twitch of a smile as he emerged on to the hotel terrace. Faced by his tall, impassive presence, Eleanor, out of breath and dishevelled, began to feel slightly foolish. The whirl of panic-fuelled action following her conversation with Sofia suddenly began to seem slightly hysterical. Yan's searching appraisal made her abruptly aware of her tense, stressed condition.

'Eleanor, what is wrong?' Firmly he took hold of her shoulders. Humorous curiosity tilted his dark eyebrows. 'What has happened? I suggested you swim, sunbathe and relax. Did you instead decide to go jogging, in one hundred degrees of heat?'

'No. I... Sofia called round...' She swallowed on a bitter lump in her throat. Trembling with anger and apprehension, she found herself quite unable to go on.

'Sofia?' he echoed, blankly amused. 'Did Sofia suggest that you go jogging, perhaps?'

'No. She...she said some things that...that I have to talk to you about...'

There was a short, charged silence. Then with some indecipherable but none too polite-sounding comment in Greek, Yan steered her through the

lounge area, where visitors took refuge from the
intense sun to laze around playing backgammon or
drinking or reading, towards the private stairs up
to his apartment. At the top landing he pushed her
firmly through the heavy oak door, and closed it
firmly behind them.

Without any warning, the past sprang instantly
to agonising life.

She caught her breath on a ragged gulp. The
painfully familiar surroundings felt like the last
straw. The navy and green furnishings had been
changed. There was a new colour scheme in deep
violet and cream, with splashes of dark apricot. But
the furniture was the same: comfortable squashy
sofas, polished beech floors, luxurious antique furniture and exotic plants. And the view was the
same—that uninterrupted vista of sea and sky and
rocky pine-covered coast. The memories were
marching back with such merciless speed that
Eleanor felt overwhelmed by too many turbulent
emotions at once, and too distraught to handle any
of them.

Sinking on to one of the striped cream and
apricot sofas, she hid her face in shaking hands.

'Eleanor...' Yan had come to squat in front of
her, his voice now devoid of humour. 'Go and take
a shower, revive yourself. I will get you a drink.'

'I don't want a shower; I want to talk to you...!'

'Then would you rather collapse from heat
exhaustion?'

Surrendering, she allowed him to usher her into
the large, mahogany-panelled bathroom. Breathing
erratically, she locked the door carefully behind her,

and leaned there for a while, eyes closed. Yan was right. She was on the point of collapse. It wasn't just running in the heat. She blamed the intense nervous strain of the last forty-eight hours, with Sofia's frightening predictions crowning the nightmare.

She had to calm down, get a grip on herself. Dutifully she peeled off her clothes, switched on the shower, and stepped beneath the powerful jets of water.

It was wonderfully refreshing. Closing her eyes again, she slowly soaped herself, with something which smelled sensuously of magnolia. The tepid water cascaded over her, cooling her throat, breasts and armpits, running rivulets down the hot plane of her stomach and thighs.

The tingling contrast was intense as she stepped out and dried herself on a thick fluffy blue towel. Energy was thankfully seeping back.

Towelling herself dry, she saw that her reflection in the long, mahogany-framed mirror on the wall resembled a stranger's. The creamy-olive skin, slender, rounded limbs, high, full breasts and narrow hips might belong to someone else entirely. For a few seconds she paused, staring at herself. What, she wondered miserably, had Yan ever seen in her four years ago? What, from his viewpoint, could possibly have triggered that short, heady spell of sensual hunger? Her brown hair was long and thick, but such an ordinary brown, so very ordinary. Her figure was fairly unremarkable, as far as she could judge. Not too fat, nor too thin, but not spectacular and curvaceous and sexy like

Sofia's... Her eyes were large and deep-set and thick-lashed, and quite a strong, brilliant shade of bluey-green, but her jaw was too square, her cheekbones too high, her nose too *retroussé*...

Turning away impatiently, she tore out the hair band restraining her hair, found a large tortoiseshell brush and applied it vigorously, then pulled her clothes back on, averting her eyes from her shortcomings. No use worrying about things you couldn't change. That was the kind of homily her mother had been fond of trotting out in moments of personal crisis. Remembering it made her feel slightly more sad, but strangely comforted...

Emerging a few minutes later, barefoot, carrying her sandals, she found Yan in the shining white kitchen, brewing coffee. He levelled a penetrating inspection at her.

'You look better.'

'Yes. Thanks. I do feel cooler...'

'Good.' Yan's dark eyes were bland as he led the way into the sitting area, with its sweeping view. 'Come and have some coffee. Milk, no sugar? Do I remember correctly?'

'Yes... how clever of you to remember.' She found it hard to keep the irony from her voice.

'You may be surprised to know how many things I remember about you, Eleanor.'

Dropping her eyes, taking a sip of coffee, she tensed slightly.

'Yan, I didn't come here to take a nostalgic trip into the past. Something Sofia said today has made me feel very angry and very... frightened...'

'And what did Sofia say to you, Eleanor?' His voice and his expression were deadpan.

'I have to know the truth.' Her throat dried as she looked up and caught the narrowed, unfathomable darkness of Yan's gaze. 'You say we must get married. But that, I know, is just your... misguided sense of honour all over again...'

'Eleanor...' There was a warning note in the deep voice, but she rushed on.

'Please let me finish. I've told you that I cannot marry you. Now I need to know exactly where I stand, Yan. You wouldn't try to keep Christophor here, in Greece? You wouldn't be planning on trying to take him away from me?'

Yan said nothing. He was sprawled lazily on the end of the sofa, and his dark gaze was coolly dispassionate.

'Is that what Sofia said I would do?' he queried at last.

'That... was the gist of her remarks, yes...'

'And what would I do then, I wonder?' He sounded ominously bland, his emotions unfathomable. 'Marry Sofia, of course. And think of some convenient way to dispose of you? Have you flogged for disobedience? Deported? Bribe the Greek government to refuse you re-entry to the country? Perhaps I could have you framed as an international terrorist and flung into jail?'

'I don't think being *facetious* is going to help this discussion——' she began stiffly, then stopped abruptly as Yan, without warning, swiftly closed the safe gap between them to take hold of her in a steely grip. The gleam in his eyes was a disturbing mixture of grim amusement and suppressed anger.

'What a power-crazed monster I am reputed to be,' he drawled softly. 'Your hero Apollo had nothing on me, did he? I would stop at nothing to get my own way; is that it, Eleanor? No action could be deemed too mean or ruthless to be attributed to me?'

Apollo wasn't mean and ruthless, she thought distractedly. He was supposed to represent the warmth of the sun. He was the god of prophesy, of art, music, poetry, the intellect...Comparing Yan with Apollo had seemed to fit when their relationship had been warm and loving. Now it seemed hopelessly inaccurate and naïve...

'Yan...' Her voice was a faint choke in her throat as he jerked her, abruptly, against his chest and closed hard arms around her to trap her there. Confused, bewildered by the way she'd been flung neatly into the wrong yet again, she began to speak and found her mouth covered by Yan's, in a kiss that grew in hunger and urgency.

'Yan, please...' It was a muffled protest, the last she was capable of. Heat erupted, engulfed her, so powerfully unexpected in the circumstances that she seemed to have no way of fighting it. She tried, but it seemed as if her limbs were weighted...

'Eleanor...don't fight me...' The husky, masterful command made the fine down of hair at her nape prickle into life, sent shivers of agonised longing down her spine. When he moved his hands to stroke and caress the smoothness of her back through the navy silk of her blouse, she tensed and then shuddered in despairing need.

'Don't do this...' It was her voice saying the words, but conviction seemed to have deserted her. Instead of galvanising every muscle in her body to kick and punch and free herself, she was allowing hot streaks of sensation to turn her limbs to water, allowing lean, seeking fingers access to the silk of her bare flesh beneath the blouse, writhing involuntarily as buttons were unfastened and zips dispensed with.

He covered her mouth, deepening the kiss as he undid the frothy peach lace of her bra. With a tense shiver, she felt him pull it away from the full, creamy swell of her breasts. When he took his mouth from her lips and dropped his head to gaze at the soft, exposed curves, she jerked her hands to cover herself. With hungry insistence, he took her hands away, moving his mouth to trail kisses of fire around the sensitive aureola, then to suckle at each hotly pointed carmine-pink nipple. She could only gasp for air and tremble at the force of the sensations rocking her whole body.

'Oh, *Yan*...' The sob was torn from her. Raking desperate fingers through the thickness of his black hair, she closed her eyes, let her head fall back so far that she felt her hair brushing heavily against the base of her spine. Then she collapsed helplessly back against the softness of the sofa, pressed there by Yan's controlled, determined weight.

'Do you remember how it was that first time?' The hoarse whisper was half mocking, yet thicker with desire.

As he softly spoke, he was slipping her shorts down, peeling the modest covering of peach lace with them. The cool breeze from the ceiling fan touched her nakedness, but her eyes were locked with Yan's; it was Yan's taut, possessive gaze which made her shiver.

'The way we fell on each other like two starving strangers finding a banquet?' he continued roughly, half under his breath, as he traced a searing trail of kisses from her throat to her groin. 'I had never wanted any woman the way I wanted you, Eleanor...and nothing has changed, *agapití mou*...'

It was a harsh groan. With fiercely impatient stripping motions he flung off his shirt and jerked a hand to the belt of his jeans, levering himself up from her in a ripple of tanned muscle and devastating male beauty.

Dimly, in some distant lonely corner of her mind, Eleanor acknowledged to herself that this had gone too far, that if she let this go on she would be lost, that she might slip off the tracks into the wilderness and be lost forever...

'Yan...' The pain cracking in her voice jolted a reaction in his eyes, but he didn't release her. Instead he crushed her beneath him with barely restrained savagery, with a shudder of emotion which couldn't help but communicate his urgency.

'That was why I could not believe you were *parthènos*,' he breathed against her lips, his caresses subtly slowing to take her with him on his erotic spiral of desire, his tongue delving deeply between her lips to fence with hers, his fingers cupping and moulding her breasts, grazing and gently pinching her nipples with a skill which left her gasping and writhing with sensation, then stroking lower to explore the tell-tale moistness between her legs with a bold bravura which brooked no resistance, 'why I took you with such roughness, sweet Eleanor, when I should have been patient and tender...'

'Please, Yan...' she sobbed, beside herself now. She was burning up, lost to reason, aflame with a spinning liquid fire as his expert fingers probed and affirmed and triumphantly stormed the small, shy involuntary clenching of her muscles in her most intimate place, letting her arms go round his neck in bitter, intoxicated submission.

'I hate you for this,' she whispered raggedly, her lips discovering the coarse five o'clock shadow of his jaw. 'I hate myself, but if you don't make love to me now I think I'll die...'

There was a moment of total stillness, a tense, wordless, motionless pause, like being in the eye of a storm. She could feel the strength of his arousal, powerfully hard against the softness of her stomach. The force of his need sent shivers of sensation rippling through her, bringing goose-bumps to her thighs and back. Then, to her shocked disbelief, he suddenly pulled away from her, with a fierce, frustrated groan. Every muscle and sinew of his body seemed to be thrown into savage relief as he levered himself to one side and then sat hunched, shuddering violently, elbows on tautly powerful thighs, head in hands.

'Sweet *hell*, Eleanor...' The words were forced through his teeth. With ferocious strength he sprang to his feet and strode across to the bathroom, slamming the door with angry finality.

As if on a distant planet, she huddled in humiliation on the sofa. She heard the shower running. Disbelief, disillusion, self-disgust ... she couldn't even begin to decide which reaction took precedence over the other.

By the time Yan emerged, black hair wet and slicked back, dark eyes bleak, a calf-length dark blue towelling bathrobe belted purposefully around his waist, she'd summoned sufficient impetus to pull on her clothes.

She stared at him in silence.

'Don't look at me like that,' he recommended grimly, retrieving his clothes from the floor and slinging them on to a chair. 'It is at times like this when I wish I had not given up cigarettes.'

'I can't believe you just did that to me,' she said slowly, bitterly, choosing her words with care. 'It really is all about *revenge*, isn't it? This whole thing ...'

'No, Eleanor ...' He sounded clipped, angry, inexpressibly weary, as he sank into a chair at a safe distance. 'It is not.'

'Then what *is* your excuse?' she ground out. She'd never felt so agitated, so totally shredded inside. She ached, burned, winced with conflicting desires and emotions. How *could* he have done that? Assaulted her senses, dragged her to the very peak of submission and desire, goaded her into begging him to make love to her, and then stepped back ... demonstrated eleventh-hour self-control ...?
He *was* a monster ...

'If you ask me what this is all about...' he said slowly. The deep voice rang with suppressed emotion, she realised bleakly. Yan was feeling *something*, then. He wasn't totally devoid of human feeling... 'It's about making sense of the past, Eleanor.'

She stared at him, her heart still thumping at twice its normal rate.

'The past made perfect sense to me,' she said at last in a small voice. 'You were engaged to your cousin Sofia. You met me, recognised an easy push-over when you saw one. You fancied a... a quick summer affair... a last fling before tying yourself down, maybe? One which would conveniently reach its natural termination when I went back to England after the summer tourist season——'

'Eleanor...' Yan's interruption was hoarsely angry, but she ploughed on.

'Then Laura told you I was pregnant. So all your fierce national pride and... and misguided sense of honour came roaring to the rescue. Solely because I was carrying *your* child, you decided to turn a meaningless summer romance into a permanent, lifelong commitment!'

'Meaningless?' Yan echoed grimly. There was a glitter of banked-down fury in his dark eyes. It made her pause for breath in her volley of accusation. 'You can sit there and tell me that what we had together was *meaningless*?' He bit out the words in a clipped, incredulous voice.

'All right... I admit I was fairly "wrapped up" in you at the time,' she admitted shakily. 'But——'

'You, my darling Eleanor, were impulsive, over-romantic and totally blinkered.' The drawled taunt was bitterly humorous, but it brought a flame of reaction to her face.

'Thanks. Nothing like compliments to make a girl feel good about herself.'

There was another tight silence.

'I was the realist. You were the romantic. You saw life like a fairy-story, and waited for a happy ending. Life isn't like that, Eleanor. Every life has a sad ending,' Yan said at last, in a cool, contemplative voice. 'We are born, we live our allotted span, and then we die. It is what we choose to do with our lives while we have the chance. That is the important thing...'

She stared at him, her stomach clenching in anguished awareness. She thought with abrupt pain of her parents' lives. Of her shock when her mother died, of finding letters from a father she'd been bitterly informed had died years before...

If only their story could have had the fairy-tale ending it deserved, she reflected miserably. And if only her own passionate commitment to Yan had been fully returned.

'Christophor is my happy ending,' she said quietly, with a wry, choked laugh. 'Whatever pain we caused each other, Yan, having Christophor is the greatest joy I have ever known.'

The darkening of his eyes told her she'd said the wrong thing.

'Which makes my deprivation all the more unforgivable, don't you agree?' he queried with soft accusation.

'At the time it was the only way I could think of to get away from Greece, and from you...' She clenched her fists at her sides. She'd meant to strike back at him, but she hadn't foreseen the surge of pain in his eyes.

'To get away from Greece? And from me?' he echoed flatly, the deep lines from nose to mouth hardening cynically. 'And now you have the nerve to beg me not to take Christophor from you? When you have already committed the crime in reverse, Eleanor?'

She felt the blood drain from her face.

'Are you telling me what Sofia said was true?' she whispered, standing up with an immense effort. 'That you *would* stoop to trying to take my child away from me, Yan?'

There was a fierce silence. Their eyes locked, brilliant jade with deep-set coal-black.

'Stay here in Greece. Do the honourable thing, Eleanor. Marry me,' Yan taunted, cool steel in his voice. 'Then you will not have to worry about such an eventuality, will you?'

CHAPTER FIVE

THE white sand, in the fierce late morning sun, was unbearably hot. It was impossible to walk on it with bare feet. Consumed with an acute anxiety attack after yesterday's events, feeling illogically threatened and over-protective, Eleanor kept Christophor to the shade of the pine-covered cliffs, where he could dig and paddle and sail in the small rubber dinghy left for him by Evangelie's small nephew.

There'd been no sign of Yan either last night or this morning. Whether he was deliberately giving her a breathing space, or whether he genuinely had business to attend to, he must have spent the night at his hotel apartment. Probably with Sofia, she thought acidly, thinking of the proprietorial way the other girl had touched his shoulder at lunch yesterday...

She sat, cross-legged in the sand, clad in brief jade Lycra swimsuit, watching Christophor solemnly paddling his small craft backwards and forwards, deeply engrossed in one of his solitary childhood make-believe games.

Someone to talk to would be nice, she reflected bleakly, looping the dinghy's safety rope more securely around her wrist, smiling and waving back as Christophor flapped a chubby hand at her. Someone to help her as she struggled to make sense of her feelings.

She should ring Geoffrey, she knew. He'd be wondering what was going on. On several occasions she'd picked up the telephone to dial his number in England, and then changed her mind. Dear, solid, dependable Geoffrey. He represented the straightforward, trustworthy sort of man she should have met before that passionate fiasco with Yan. Passionate wasn't a word one would apply to Geoffrey. But good, and kind, and sensible, if just a fraction on the pompous side . . . they were words which could describe him.

So why didn't she ring him for advice now? She didn't know, she confessed miserably to herself. Unless it was because she'd fallen violently under Yan's autocratic spell again, after only two days here in Greece . . .

She strained sand absently through her fingers. Yan had always had the ability to cast a spell over her. It seemed nothing much had changed, despite the four-year interval . . .

Chewing her lip distractedly, Eleanor gazed at the violet horizon, her eyes cloudy with painful memories. She'd blacked it all out of her mind for so long that it felt like a physical pain to recall those long-ago fateful few weeks, leading on from that critical turning-point in her life when Yan had made love to her for the very first time . . .

As he'd taunted yesterday, she'd been a virgin. That experience with Yan, in the magical enclosed cocoon of his hotel apartment, had knocked her sideways, tipped her world to a crazy angle, distorted her normal common sense, transformed an independent, innocent, intelligent twenty-one-year-

old into a woman whose entire existence, whose
whole reason for being, revolved around a man.

An intense, involuntarily contraction tightened
her stomach, just thinking about that first time. As
Yan had so cynically put it last night, they'd 'fallen
on each other like two starving strangers finding a
banquet'. The emotion driving them together had
resulted in a rushed, hectic, almost incoherent
fusion of bodies, minds and, for Eleanor at least,
souls.

'Sweet little Eleanor ... I could lose my mind ...'
he'd whispered, his voice ragged with anguished
resignation as he'd undressed her, lifted her into his
arms, and carried her to his room, casually dis-
carding the towel which covered his hips.

'You *make* me lose my mind ...' The deep voice
had held a thick ache of desire as he'd laid her on
his bed, feasting his dark gaze on the slender legs
and high young breasts. But it had been she who'd
lost her mind, sucked into the hot, dark vortex of
sensation, experiencing emotions she'd never
dreamed of before. With self-constraint, he'd put
his own explosive desires on hold as he aroused her
to sensual awareness, kissed every inch of her body,
caressed and explored and moulded every curve and
hollow, and finally, when the tornado of desire was
so violent that neither could hold out against it,
when his hoarse breathing and murmured words of
love had wound her emotions up to fever-pitch,
when she was whimpering with pleasure and need
and impatience, he'd relinquished control. He'd
pinned her wide open beneath his muscled strength,

and thrust with ruthless, agonised tenderness into
that tight, delicate core of her femininity...

He'd been shattered to discover she was a virgin.
Her tense recoil, the widening of her eyes, her sharp
hissed intake of breath, brought the whole experience juddering to an incredulous halt.

'Is it possible? Can you be *parthènos*? Virgin?'
he'd groaned unsteadily. The deep voice had been
thick with carnal emotion and arousal, but his dark
face had twisted with gentle humour and remorse.
'Have I dragged a little virgin into my bed, Eleanor?
And not even noticed?'

'It's not funny, Yan,' she'd choked, with a shiver
of fear, desire and deep, surging adoration as she
gazed up at him.

'No, it is serious,' he'd said softly, suppressed
desire aching in his voice. 'And it is madness,
Eleanor... too risky, if you are a virgin...'

'Just...just *do* it,' she'd whispered, heat flooding
her whole body as well as her face at the answering
glitter of triumphant laughter in his eyes.

'Just *do* it?' he'd teased thickly, dropping his
head to plunder her soft mouth with his tongue,
gathering her to him with a fierce surge of tenderness. 'What an elegant way to invite a man to
take your most precious possession, Miss Eleanor
Carrington...'

'Oh, Yan...' She'd been half laughing, half
sobbing as she clung to him. 'I sometimes think I
must be the only twenty-one-year-old virgin in the
universe! And I love you! I love you so much...'

Crushed together again, chest, stomach and
thighs in fiery contact, the hunger and arousal of

the moment, the urgent need to finish what had
been started, combined with her husky declaration
of love, had been too great for Yan. With abrupt,
savage expertise, he had taken what was offered to
him. Tumbled ecstatically on the wide blue-silk-
covered bed, with the sound of the strong *meltémi*
wind moaning in the pines beyond the open
windows, she'd given herself to Yan Diamakis with
all the healthy, joyous enthusiasm of the very young
and deeply in love . . .

. . . and deeply stupid, Eleanor reflected now,
wincing in remembered agony as she thought of that
passionate, indiscreet avowal. How could she have
blurted out her feelings like that? How could she
ever have been so gullible?

Something Yan had said yesterday returned to
taunt her. She'd been very sure of what she wanted,
he'd said. She'd been single-minded. Blinkered.
And she hadn't changed. Was that true? Was that
the way she was? The way Yan saw her?

Christophor had been conceived that very first
night. After that hot, crazy eruption of physical
desire between them, unpremeditated and foolishly
unprotected, Yan had been meticulous, responsible
and commendably mature about their sexual relationship. He'd taken precautions, gone to every
length to protect her. But it had been too late. And
the summer weeks had drifted by in a heady bubble
of loving and wanting, of water-ski lessons and
candlelit tavernas and nights dancing under the
stars . . . until Yan had gone to Athens on business,
and Sofia's family had closed ranks and spelled out
the truth . . .

At least, she reflected with wry sadness, she could feel that her child had been conceived in love and laughter and tenderness . . .

Yet now she had to contemplate exposing him to tension, bitterness and emotional upheaval . . .

Jumping to her feet, she waded into the clear aquamarine shallows, plunged into the silky coolness, and swam out to join Christophor at the dinghy.

'How's the little sailor?' she teased gently. 'Is there room for Mummy in your boat?'

Christophor examined the confined space, and slowly shook his head.

'Never mind. I'll just have to swim alongside . . .'

'There is room for both of you in mine,' Yan said, startling her as he swam up behind. He trapped her against his body beneath the water, strong arms on either side as he held the dinghy. The body contact sent shivers of awareness coursing through her bloodstream.

'Papa!' Christophor's greeting was transparently delighted. At least there was one uncomplicated person around here, Eleanor reflected, suppressing her turmoil for the child's sake.

'Get a change of clothes, and we'll go out on the launch for the day,' Yan said, coolly decisive.

As she glared at him, he grinned and dived beneath the water again and surfaced at the other side of the dinghy.

'Is that meant to be a polite invitation?' she enquired blankly. 'Because if so, it sounded more like an order!'

'Forgive me, Eleanor,' he mocked unrepentantly, beginning to tow the boat, with Christophor inside it, towards the shore. 'Let's see if we can spend the rest of the day enjoying the company of our son, shall we?'

Put that way, she thought resentfully, following him out of the water and retreating to the house with as much dignity as she could raise, it was an offer she couldn't possibly refuse...

The Aegean was calm as sapphire silk as the powerful launch nosed its way lazily around the coast. Christophor, life-jacketed and buckled to a safety-line, was ecstatically clambering up and down the bench seats in the cockpit. Yan, cool and casual in cream cotton bermudas and collarless white shirt, eyes hidden behind black-lensed sunglasses, talked to him, let him steer, and answered his solemn list of questions about what, where, why and how everything worked. He was a natural father, Eleanor was forced to acknowledge, huddled in the corner of the bench seat in jade culottes and sea-blue T-shirt. He radiated warmth, approval, humour and patience. His enjoyment of the child was totally unforced. Liking children wasn't something you could pretend...

Unbidden, an image of Geoffrey sprang to mind, suffering Christophor's presence until the blessed relief of bedtime. It made such a stark contrast with this joyous rapport between father and son that it almost took her breath away.

'You're unusually quiet today.' Yan glanced at her obliquely, mockery tilting his mouth.

'Perhaps after what happened between us yesterday, I'm not feeling especially sociable.'

'*Endaxi*. But what should I apologise for?' He tilted a wry glance at her again, over his shoulder. 'For what did happen? Or for what didn't happen?'

'You think you're so damn clever, don't you? Using that great technique of yours to prove something to yourself?'

'Didn't it prove something to you as well?' he queried softly.

Heat flared in her face. 'It just reminded me how it all began, yes!' she admitted with quiet anger. 'And it reminded me what a vast difference there is between love, and sexual desire!'

'So...the romantic has woken up to reality?' he taunted cruelly, after a slight pause.

'Oh, yes, Yan,' she agreed woodenly, averting her eyes from his. 'Reality has never seemed more vivid.'

'So you're going to fight me to the end?'

To what end? she wondered in fierce, anguished silence. To the end which left a small child torn helplessly between two warring adults?

She rubbed her forehead with a shaking hand.

'Whatever you might think, I don't want to fight you all the time,' she said slowly. 'When I wrote to you, I half hoped we could just sit down like two mature adults and work out how you could take some responsibility in Christophor's upbringing...'

'Ah. I see. ''Responsibility'' here is a euphemism for no-strings financial support?'

Her temper flared again, and she doggedly fought for calm. Why was he deliberately goading her?

'No. I'm self-sufficient financially, thank you.'

'And "Geoffrey"? No doubt he has plenty of money too.'

'Yes. He's comfortably off.' Irritation flared. Somewhere in the depths of her heart, she was cursing ever mentioning Geoffrey's name. 'Could you please stop bringing Geoffrey into every conversation?' she snapped, involuntarily.

One dark eyebrow tilted in sardonic surprise. 'Whatever you wish.'

'I...I'd much rather discuss Sofia,' she added, gathering courage. 'I must confess I'm a little surprised you two didn't get married.'

There was a silence. They were passing the furthest tip of the island, rounding the glorious Koukounariés Beach with its banks of soft green pines growing down nearly to the water's edge. Eleanor gazed but hardly saw, too tense to appreciate the beauty of their surroundings.

'That question,' he said at last, 'sums up how little you ever understood about our relationship, doesn't it? For someone so intelligent, you have a remarkably obtuse nature, Eleanor.'

'Why must you always evade my questions?' she persisted quietly. 'And how can you pretend that you weren't in love with her? You were scheduled to marry her in the autumn, when you met me that summer, weren't you? You didn't tell me, because you knew it would wreck your chances of a spot of light-hearted sex with me while Sofia and her family were away on their annual visit to Italy. You can't tell me that's not true, because you *know* it's true...'

Yan's smile was a thin parody of amusement.

'I have long ago abandoned the hope of convincing you of my integrity,' he said indifferently. 'Your favourite story of Apollo and Daphne springs to mind again, doesn't it? How no one could convince her that Apollo's love was genuine, that she had nothing to fear. How she preferred the extraordinary fate of being turned into a bay-tree, to escape from him.'

Eleanor had to smile. Yan's deadpan expression held that gleam of humour she'd always found powerfully contagious.

'As you said yourself,' she protested, her smile quickly fading, 'I'm hardly role-playing Daphne! If I were, I'd have hopped on the next boat home that summer, my chastity intact!'

'Instead,' Yan murmured implacably, 'you told me you'd miscarried our child, and then went into hiding for four years. That makes Daphne seem a warm, well-balanced female in comparison.'

'Oh, Yan...' Her voice was husky, because her throat swelled suddenly, in a surge of emotion. There was a bleak pain in Yan's deep voice which abruptly communicated itself to her, on an entirely different level from their petty sparring and bickering. 'Yan, I'm *sorry*...!'

He was very still as he stood at the wheel, the muscular width of his shoulders suddenly tense beneath the white cotton of his shirt.

'Sorry?' he echoed quietly, cynicism cutting deep lines around his mouth as he glanced down at her.

'Did you say *sorry*, Eleanor? Sorry is a word I never thought I'd hear you say.'

'You make me sound a delightful person,' she whispered unsteadily. Her fists were balled at her sides. Christophor clambered up beside her on the seat, and jumped on to her lap, and with an immense effort she controlled her trembling nerves. 'But I am sorry. I'm sorry that…that you've missed Christophor's first three years. At the time, I really had no idea how much it would—it would hurt you. It was a case of…of self-preservation, I'm afraid…'

'You had to preserve yourself from me?' he queried wryly. 'And that makes me seem a "delightful person" too, doesn't it?'

Christophor had taken off his small white sunhat, and suddenly reached up and plonked it on Eleanor's head, laughing at the result.

'Perhaps we need to call a truce,' Yan suggested wryly, watching Eleanor smiling at the small child in her arms with an unreadable glitter in his dark eyes. 'For our son's sake?'

'Yes, perhaps we do…'

'Or if not for his sake, then if only for the pleasure of seeing you laugh again. Did you know that you have enchanting dimples in your cheeks when you laugh, Eleanor?'

'Do I?' At the drily caressing note in his voice, a stubborn little glow of response had begun in her stomach. This was dangerous, stupid, idiotic…like walking blindfold into quicksand. But the temporary relief of suspending hostilities was so enormous that she almost felt the tension lift from her shoulders.

'Where are we going?' she asked quickly, to cover her confusion.

'Nowhere in particular.' Yan's gaze held hers for a long, searching moment, dropping lazily to encompass the swell of her breasts beneath the soft blue T-shirt, before he steered the boat back on course and increased their speed through the sunlit water. 'Where would you like to go?'

His dark gaze brought yesterday's near lovemaking, his humiliating rejection of her, painfully back to mind. She shrugged stiffly.

'Oh, I don't know. Anywhere . . .' Her cheeks suddenly burned again. As always, she had no idea where she stood with him. She had the feeling there was another level to their conversation. And emotionally, she had the disturbing sensation of floundering in deep water, in acute danger of drowning . . .

The feeling intensified later, when Christophor was safely back on dry land and firmly transferred by Yan to Evangelie's care.

Yan's suggestion of water-skiing, coming after the friendlier atmosphere created by their outing, was unnervingly hard to refuse. She discovered that, once learned, the skill was easily recaptured. In the golden evening sun, they spent a couple of hours slicing through the sparkling water. The lift to her spirits was unbelievable.

Laughing, breathless, she waded out after her last high-speed sweep of the bay, and collapsed next to Yan where he was lazing, watching her, on a nearby beach-bed.

'Oh, I'd forgotten how wonderful it felt,' she admitted, tingling with energy and adrenalin. 'Sport at home has been limited to sedate swimming at my hotel pool, or workouts in the gymnasium when I've time . . .'

'Whatever it is you've been doing, it has kept you in perfect shape, Eleanor.'

The dry compliment made her glance at him in surprise.

'*Efharisto*,' she murmured. 'But I'll be stiff all over tomorrow. I've discovered muscles I haven't used for years!'

'But you are near the coast, where you live in Northumberland?'

She gave a mock-shiver. 'True. But I'm a fair-weather person. Wet-suits and brisk easterly winds don't hold quite the same appeal.'

'Another good reason for staying here in Greece?' Yan's tone was light, flippant. She decided to take the comment in the same vein, and ignore it.

Glancing at him, after a brief silence, she realised that he seemed distant, his mind clearly on other things. The dark eyes looked thoughtful.

'You look preoccupied?' she queried at last.

'Business matters again,' he supplied briefly. There was a tone in his voice which implied that a mere female would have no interest in 'business matters'.

Suppressing an urge to scream, she said evenly, 'Which ones? The hotel here?'

Focusing on her properly, he nodded, his wide mouth twisting wryly at her apparent interest. 'I have to go to Athens for an important meeting tomorrow. Unfortunately the hotel staff seem to be dropping like flies. Some mystery virus.'

She stared at him. So he could ill afford all this time out? Taking Christophor out in the boat, water-skiing now with her? Somehow this knowledge touched a chord, gave her a slightly warmer feeling. The idea of Yan Diamakis making business sacrifices to achieve personal goals made her feel subtly flattered, and slightly guilty...

'So... you're wondering how the hotel is going to cope,' she sympathised.

'Correct. There are two big parties due tomorrow. One English, one German. And my manager and two of my tri-lingual receptionists have taken to their beds...'

'I could help out, if you like.' What possessed her to say it, she would never know. Catching the glimmer of surprised amusement in Yan's eyes, she had the impression he was as taken aback as she was.

'You?'

The incredulous reaction brought her motives into focus. This was a sharp desire to prove something, she admitted to herself. To demonstrate to this chauvinistic male that she was a person of some intelligence and ability. Not just an empty-headed female who happened to have borne his son...

'Why not?' she persisted calmly. How she wished she could outgrow this embarrassing habit of reddening whenever he scanned her face so closely. 'I know the basic routines here—you can't have forgotten how I used to help out that summer when we... when I...'

'When we became lovers?' he supplied wryly, his gaze kindling disturbingly on her flushed cheeks. 'So you did.'

'Yes. And these days I'm . . . I'm more experienced in hotel work. I can turn my hand to most things. And remember, I speak German quite well . . .'

He considered this proposal for an insulting length of time. Then he nodded, with a faint grin and a shrug, his eyes intently on hers.

'All right. *Efharisto*. Thank you, Eleanor. Perhaps this will be good experience for you, for when you are my wife.'

Jolted rudely out of her careful poise, she quickly covered her flare of reaction. Laugh it off, she told herself sternly. Don't take his taunts seriously.

'I hardly think so, somehow,' she laughed, a touch breathlessly, reddening even more as his gaze narrowed. 'Aren't working wives rather rare in your country? Besides, marriages of *convenience* went out with the ark, Yan!'

Behind her casual dismissal, the churning of emotions was so strong and conflicting that it made her almost dizzy. Glancing at Yan, she found herself freshly unnerved by his powerful virility, lounging beside her in brief black swimming-trunks. His limbs were lean, muscled, coarsely sprinkled with black hair. His torso was etched with hard, powerful contours, his abdomen impressively taut and flat . . .

He was so close to her that she could smell the cool, clean fragrance of his skin, with just the faintest hint of fresh perspiration. There was a dangerous silence, she realised belatedly, gathering her wayward thoughts from the distraction of his raw maleness...

'I would say I know a little more about "working wives" in my country than you do,' he pointed out drily. 'As for a "marriage of convenience"... are you suggesting what I *think* you are suggesting?'

Fists clenched behind her back, she avoided his keenly mocking stare. She had every right to make the point. Hadn't Sofia, and in the past Sofia's parents, spelled out exactly how she'd be expected to behave as the wife of Yan Diamakis? And hadn't their warnings held more than a ring of truth? Even Laura, from her worldly-wise experience, had hinted at a rigid, chauvinistic structure which a young English girl might find very hard to adapt to...

Yan's cruel amusement was hard to bear.

'Platonic marriage, do you mean?' he goaded. 'As in nothing physical? No falling on each other like starving strangers? After last night, can I be hearing right?'

She had an overpowering desire to hit him. She repressed her surge of fury with great difficulty. There was nothing to be gained from rising to his bait.

'After last night,' she pointed out with cold justice, 'I should have thought you'd be only too happy to agree. You demonstrated a strong... *distaste* for my meagre favours!'

'Is that what you think?' He shook his head slowly as he stared at her. 'Is that really what you think happened last night, Eleanor?' His eyes raked her slender body, in the jade swimsuit, and she winced at the bold gleam of knowledge she read there. To her mortification, her nipples tightened as his eyes lingered on her breasts. Beneath the tight Lycra, she felt a heat begin to prickle her skin.

'What was I supposed to think?' she shot back shakily, clutching at her pride as she folded her arms defensively. 'That you found me totally irresistible?'

'Not quite the case, I agree,' he teased. He was controlling his derision with difficulty. There was still a slight shake to his voice. How could he find this situation even remotely amusing?

She shrugged. This conversation had an air of unreality about it. Something was folding up and slowly dying inside her. To cover her embarrassment, she opened her mouth to change the subject quickly, then shut it abruptly as Yan moved closer, and she found herself hauled unceremoniously into his arms. Before she could evade him, he'd bent his dark head to kiss her, effectively silencing her with an explosion of unwanted sensation.

The kiss was explicit in its possessive demand. With hungry savagery he cupped her face with his hands, and plundered the depths of her mouth, his tongue fencing with hers in almost brutal insistence. If the sexual act could be mimicked with nothing more than a kiss, Eleanor thought dizzily, shuddering convulsively, then this was the kiss...

Sliding his fingers down from her face, he moulded her shoulders and then traced down to brush his thumbs boldly over the pointed crests of her nipples beneath the swimsuit. She tensed as a fire of sensation burned right through her.

'Forget this "marriage of convenience",' he teased huskily, breaking contact with her mouth to fiercely rake her face with a narrowed gaze. 'A marriage between us would be a marriage in every sense of the word, sweet Eleanor. Make no mistake. You would share my bed, as well as my life.'

She stared at him in riotous confusion. Yan's kiss had turned her knees to liquid, warmed her stomach. His power to arouse her was humiliating and frightening.

Could she believe what he said? Could she take that quantum leap into the dark with him, after the disaster in the past? She was frightened, she realised dimly. She didn't understand him. She didn't understand his actions last night, his last-minute rejection of her, when his desire was so real and vibrant that she could feel it shudder between them now, almost tangible...

She was totally confused, torn between the strength of her response to him, and the wisdom of resisting him. It felt like being on a see-saw of emotions, frighteningly out of control unless she exerted an exhausting amount of strength to slow it down, to keep a grip on it all...

With a huge effort, she tried to laugh off the shivers of need, shrug off the intimate tension of the moment.

'I couldn't...' she said huskily, hardly making sense. So much for laughing it off, she reflected dimly. Yan's sensual assault, his disturbing talk of marriage, of sharing his bed, had totally thrown her. Feeling the way she did right this moment, shaken and melting and inwardly on fire, how could she pretend to herself that the prospect was so awful?

But he'd said nothing about *love*. He never had. Not in the whole of that summer, four years ago. And not now. Not in so many words. How could she even begin to contemplate risking her future, and Christophor's, to a man with such power over her, who didn't *love* her? The way she still loved him...

Aghast at this mental confession, she lowered her eyes, frozen with panic. She *did* still love him. It was true, she realised, veiling her anguish behind thick brown lashes. Her mouth dry, she fought to collect herself. Like swimming against a fatal current, she finally managed to meet his eyes again. His gaze was lidded, unnervingly intent, as he watched her inner struggles.

'You couldn't...?' he probed softly.

'It wouldn't work, and you know it,' she finished, finally succeeding in striking a cooler note. 'Besides...we...we weren't discussing marriage just now, were we? We were discussing the hotel, and you agreed I could help you out... Do you still want me to?'

Taking her chin between his thumb and forefinger, his touch sending convulsive tremors right down into her stomach, he examined her hot face intently.

'*Ne*, Eleanor. Yes,' he teased gently, pulling her to her feet, his arm around her shoulders and irony in his husky voice. 'Perhaps against my better judgement, I will accept your generous offer of help.'

The kiss he dropped on her parted lips was unnervingly sensual, and held more than a hint of
masculine triumph.

She had the uncomfortable feeling, as she walked
beside him up towards the hotel, that she'd just
sealed some kind of bargain, without having the
faintest idea what it was...

CHAPTER SIX

'YOU sound most peculiar, Eleanor.' Geoffrey's slow, precise delivery echoed so clearly down the telephone line that he could have been in the next room instead of thousands of miles away in England. She had a vivid mental image of him, tall, slim, blond and handsome in a pleasing, honest, open way. It was unnerving how colourless and unreal that image seemed, with the raw power of Yan Diamakis freshly imprinted on her consciousness...

'Sorry,' she murmured guiltily, glancing across Yan's vast desk in his spacious office behind Reception, 'but you've rung me at the hotel. It's rather difficult to talk...'

'Your Aunt Meg gave me two numbers,' Geoffrey persisted, with mounting irritability. 'Some housekeeper at the first number told me to ring you here. This must be costing me a fortune!'

'Yes. It probably is,' Eleanor agreed flatly. 'Look, Geoffrey, I'm fine. There are just some things I have to sort out over here...'

'With Christophor's father?'

'That's right...'

'And what about me? You fly off to Greece without even telling me? I would have thought I deserved better treatment, Eleanor...'

'I know. I really am sorry. But...I left in a hurry.
Aunt Meg will fill you in on the sordid details, if
you're interested. Now I really have to go...'

'Eleanor, darling...' The irritation began to fade.
Geoffrey sounded warmer, more genuinely concerned about her. She felt a sharp twinge of guilt
that she didn't feel more grateful for that concern.
What was the matter with her? Geoffrey was a loyal
friend. True, she'd told a small white lie about their
being unofficially engaged. But that was only because she had never been able to bring herself to
say yes to his repeated offers of marriage. She'd
always thought it would be terribly unfair to agree
to marry Geoffrey, in spite of his assurances of a
proper family life for Christophor. Until now she'd
been unsure exactly why it would be so unfair. Now
she knew. She might not have the courage to marry
Yan, but, knowing how deeply she still loved him,
she knew there was no way she could ever marry
anyone else...

'Goodbye, Geoffrey. Thanks for the call. I appreciate your concern, honestly. But I'm OK.
I'll...I'll ring you soon.'

'I should hope so!' The hurt pride in his voice
sounded almost boyish, she reflected. And she supposed he had a right to feel hurt. Although in
fairness, she'd never given him any justification for
treating her like his private property...

Replacing the receiver, she stared unseeingly at
the computer booking confirmations on the screen
in front of her. Yan had been in Athens for four
days now. And she had a sense of slowly crumbling
under immense pressure. Not the strain of helping

at Yan's hotel. That was fine. Even though her involvement had been very much on an occasional, casual basis, being flung in at the deep end, responding well under pressure, these were her strong points. A telephone call to Aunt Meg in England, outlining the delicate situation she was caught up in, had relieved her of anxiety on the home front. Christophor was having the time of his life being spoilt by Evangelie and entertained by the housekeeper's niece and nephew.

The pressure was coming from her own vulnerability. With the unexpected challenge and stimulus of day-to-day routines of the Thessa Beach Hotel, being a sort of 'Girl Friday' either on Reception, in the office, on the catering front or dealing with the tour reps, she could feel herself being 'sucked in'. This all felt far too... right. Too tailor-made. Too... familiar. She might not be fluent in Greek, but the little she'd picked up during her time here as a rep and from her close involvement with Yan stood her in good stead. And even more useful were her obvious fluency in English and her working knowledge of German...

If she wasn't careful, she reflected, leaning back behind Yan's big walnut desk, she could forget all about the fiasco of her past with Yan, relinquish all claim to independence and pride, and become a permanent fixture...

She shivered involuntarily as the consequences of such folly filtered into her brain. If she let down her guard, reached out to Yan, she risked total involvement. And total involvement with Yan Diamakis would mean risking annihilation. Self-destruction. She would be committing emotional and spiritual suicide. She might just as well lie herself down in the centre of the main coast road between here and Skiathos Town and await certain death at the hands of the Skiathan taxi drivers . . .

Yan Diamakis was one hundred per cent untrustworthy. Experience had taught her as much. Why didn't the acknowledgment somehow quench this yearning ache inside her? Perhaps Geoffrey's diagnosis was accurate. She was behaving in a most peculiar way . . .

The computer screen flickered, and came back into focus as she made an effort to concentrate. The bookings didn't quite add up, she registered, with a jolt back to full concentration. Frowning at the numbers, she had an uneasy feeling that one of the hotelier's nightmares had just taken place. With the strange practice of allocating a higher number of rooms than the hotel actually possessed, shared out among the various tour companies in different countries, it was an occupational hazard. They were overbooked. Just for one night. If her hunch was correct, some unlucky couple were due to arrive this afternoon, all the way from Düsseldorf, having booked a fortnight at the Thessa Beach Hotel, only to find themselves bedless . . .

It was a hectic period. Consultation with the still groggy manager verified Eleanor's fears. A frantic reorganisation proved fruitless. The crisis was resolved by finding an excellent alternative room at another, four-star hotel a little further up the coast. By the time the unsuspecting guests arrived, the

Thessa Beach had at least some ammunition with which to defuse a potential time-bomb...

Eleanor had just managed to appease the two unlucky guests, using all the charm she could muster, as Yan appeared through the wide swing-doors of the hotel entrance. It was early evening, and he looked weary and slightly haggard, light suit jacket slung over a shoulder, sleeves of his white silk shirt pushed to the elbows, tie loosened. Smiling a parting smile at the German couple, who were to be driven to the alternative hotel in the Thessa Beach minibus, with champagne to await them in their temporary accommodation, Eleanor felt her heart miss a beat at the sight of Yan's dark, harsh face. The dark eyebrows tilted enquiringly as he watched the little scenario.

'An overbooking?' he queried bluntly. Yan's German was every bit as fluent as her own. In fact he surpassed her in his mastery of languages. She knew he could add French, Italian, Spanish and English to his list of total fluency.

She quickly explained her strategy, and earned a slow nod of approval.

'You coped well,' he commented wryly, his eyes scanning her slender form in neat cream belted cotton dress, low-heeled tan court shoes, hair wound into a shiny French plait. 'You deserve a night off, by way of celebration, Eleanor.'

'Do I?' She met his smile warily. 'OK, I accept,' she heard herself say, deeply ironic.

'Good.' His smile was equally wary, she thought. 'Go and have a swim, a bath, pamper yourself a

little. I'll come and pick up up in about an hour.
Endaxi?'

'You mean, you're proposing to take me out?'
she murmured, hiding her surprise.

'To dinner. Of course. What did you think I
meant?'

'That I needn't work the late shift tonight?' Her
needling tone drew a narrowed glimmer of
amusement.

'Have you been under such pressure, Eleanor?'
he murmured softly. 'Forgive me. I did not plan to
take advantage of your good nature.'

'I'm joking really. I've just helped out where
necessary,' she admitted quickly. 'I've had plenty
of free time to swim and play with Christophor...'

'That's good,' he confirmed smoothly. 'I am
looking forward very much to seeing my son again.
Even four days away from him have been a wrench.'

She stared at him, battling with a surge of illogical resentment. What was he subtly telling her?
That there was no way he could ever be parted from
his son? Her heart jerked and then plummeted
crazily. He was insidiously piling on the pressure.
Loading on the guilt. Psychological warfare.
Something he appeared to excel in...

The same thought was circling in her head as she
sat beside him at the bar of the small beach taverna,
where he'd brought her for a pre-dinner drink. Yan
didn't just excel in psychological warfare, he ex-
celled in the suave, sophisticated seduction technique. After a glass of *ouzo*, and half an hour of
Yan's intent questioning about her exploits at the
hotel, and an entertaining account of his trip to

Athens, she had to make an effort to remember that she was on the defensive.

'You look very...attractive tonight, Eleanor.' The wry voice brought shivers to her skin as he cast that glittering appraisal over her. 'Did you miss me while I was gone?'

'Would it boost your inflated ego if I said yes?' she countered sweetly, crossing her legs, then wishing she hadn't. On the high bar stool, the short skirt of her pink silk dress revealed a little too much newly tanned thigh for her peace of mind.

'Immeasurably.' He smiled, eyeing the revealed thigh. 'You look well, Eleanor. You've found some time to relax in the sun. That's good.'

'Oh, apart from the odd hour in the hotel here and there, I've done nothing but lie on the beach the whole four days,' she agreed calmly.

'Indeed?' Yan's dark eyes were smiling warily into hers. 'And yet my manager informs me that you have been a pillar of strength, that you have thrown yourself into helping in the hotel as if it were your own business.'

She coloured a little at the warmth of the compliment.

'Did he?'

'And overhearing the way you handled that German couple this evening, I can only believe his verdict.'

'Well, thanks for the approval,' she dimpled, drinking a little more *ouzo* and feeling the treacherous glow beginning deep in her stomach.

'Add to this Evangelie's insistence that you have spent hours playing with Christophor, and I find myself in awe of this Superwoman at my side.'

The trace of sarcasm was softened by Yan's humorous grin. But Eleanor stiffened slightly.

'It sounds to me as if you've been trotting round checking up on me!' she said, a note of indignation sharpening her voice. 'Of all the nerve...!'

Yan's amusement deepened. 'If I have, it is because I half expected you to have run away again, Eleanor.'

She glared at him over her *ouzo*, sea-green eyes simmering with mounting disbelief and anger.

'Really? I imagined your opinion of me couldn't drop much lower. Yet you think I'd offer to help you out in a crisis, and then desert you behind your back?'

He inclined his head, gravely apologetic.

'Forgive me,' he murmured solemnly. 'I can see my suspicious nature was ill-founded, Eleanor. But you will admit to lacking a track record of honesty...?'

Jumping down off the bar stool, she swung away from him, hardly trusting herself to reply. Marching furiously down the wooden steps and on to the beach, she found herself practically running to escape from him. When he easily caught up with her, and pulled her to a standstill, she was breathing as heavily as if she'd sprinted in a race.

'Eleanor, wait——'

'Let go of me...' she snapped huskily.

'For the love of the gods...' The dry growl of impatience accompanied forceful imprisonment in his arms. Despite her rigid antagonism she found herself being kissed, with a savage insistence which devastated her defences.

'Eleanor...' As he lifted the hardness of his mouth from hers, she tried to wriggle free again, but found herself trapped even tighter. One strong hand held her head, tilting her face up for merciless inspection; the other clamped her waist. The pressure between their lower bodies was raising the temperature between them to an unbearable degree. Warm, traitorous stirrings resulted in her stomach. She loathed him for his ability to raid her senses, turn anger into desire.

'Calm down,' he advised softly, restricting her freedom of movement even further by tautening the steely embrace. The heat between their tightly moulded bodies was intense now. Desire smouldered between them, irrespective of their differences. The sensual gleam swirling in the darkness of his eyes was unbearable.

'No, I will not calm down,' she spat fiercely, thumping at his shoulders. 'You accuse me of dishonesty? After your deceit over Sofia? You make me so angry, I could kill you...'

A dark eyebrow angled mockingly. 'Not here, *agapití mou*. In full view of our audience in the beach bar?'

Glancing over his shoulder, she saw what he meant. Smiling faces—holiday-makers and waiters—were witnessing the entire drama, clearly enjoying the unexpected titillation over their early evening drinks.

'I suppose you're enjoying performing for spectators,' she said through her teeth, burning with mortification at the picture they must make, the victor and the vanquished . . .

'Are you going to let me go?' she persisted shakily.

'Only when you promise me to behave. We are going into Skiathos Town for a meal,' he explained calmly, dropping another provocative kiss on her parted lips. 'And then we are going to my uncle's taverna, to watch the Greek dancing. Do you remember how we used to enjoy that, Eleanor?'

'No.'

'Then try.'

The iron clasp of his arms was no joke, she realised, with a shiver of furious resentment. Yan's strength was effortless, but physically she was totally in his power.

'All right. I remember,' she spat unsteadily. 'Now let me go . . .'

'That's better.' Carefully he eased the pressure, sliding a determined arm around her shoulders to steer her up the beach, away from the onlookers. 'Smile, Eleanor,' he advised, his deep voice full of laughter, as they drew level with the bar.

With sweet obedience she curved her mouth into a parody of a smile. Yan dropped another kiss on her lips, a silent seal of triumph. Suddenly a ripple of applause came from the beach bar, a muted call of 'Bravo'. Eleanor had to grit her teeth ferociously to prevent herself from grinding to a halt and kicking Yan hard in the shins . . .

He took her to the taverna where they'd eaten that first night, four years ago, the night she'd sat, starry-eyed and lovestruck, hanging on his every word.

'The venue is the same,' Yan commented wryly, seeing her frozen mask of politeness across the table as he glanced down the menu. 'But the atmosphere is sadly different, is it not?'

'What did you expect? After what you said to me at the beach bar. After the way you treated me just now on the beach.'

'You must learn not to over-react,' he advised with a twist of a smile, the dark gaze unrepentant. 'I accused you of nothing that was not partially true. There was no need to walk out on me . . .'

'I walked out of the beach bar because you insulted me.'

'There is always justification for your actions, isn't there, Eleanor? Just as you ran away from me four years ago because you were convinced I'd deceived you.'

'Hadn't you?'

He expelled his breath wearily.

'How many times do you need me to say this?' he said, as if abruptly reaching the end of his tether. 'I asked you to marry me because I wanted to. The baby was merely the . . . incentive to make the commitment, Eleanor . . .'

'Well, forgive me if I don't find that explanation entirely *credible*,' she countered sweetly. 'I've seen how obsessed you are with Christophor, now that you've been informed of his existence——'

'It seems to me that a man cannot win here,' Yan
cut in coolly. 'If he is callous and uninterested in
the conception and birth of his own child, he's an
uncaring chauvinist. If he cares passionately, he's
an obsessive. Someone to be escaped from at any
cost?'

Eleanor stared at him, suddenly sucked into that
vacuum of emotion which excluded the outside
world, drew every atom of her attention to the man
opposite, in casual black shirt and cream trousers,
who seemed physically close but mentally a million
light-years away. Alongside the harbourfront restaurant, the crowds milled by, their pace lazily relaxed as they enjoyed the cooler evening air,
displaying designer clothes and exotic jewellery.
Beneath the striped blue awning and pergola of vine
leaves, the candle on their white-clothed table was
a creamy pink, and in the glow Yan's dark face was
chiselled into hard angles and shadows.

He looked self-contained, shuttered in his cool
amusement. But hadn't there been real pain in his
voice, beneath the defensive sarcasm? Her heart
twisted involuntarily. Yan's recent accusations
floated back to her—single-minded, blinkered . . .
was that how she was? Was she so proud and fearful
of getting hurt that she failed to see things from
another's viewpoint?

The waiter had arrived to take their order. The
next few minutes were occupied in choosing food
and wine. Suddenly hungry, Eleanor picked tara-
mosalata, followed by souvlaki and rice.

'I will have the *dolmádhes*,' Yan said, handing
the menu to the waiter, 'and the roast chicken.'

'Yan,' she began, when they were alone again, 'you said . . . recently . . . you would never understand my reasons for lying to you about the baby . . .' Clearing her dry throat, she paused for courage, then forged on, 'But at the time, everything seemed wrong. Frightening, and wrong.'

'Frightening?' The derision cut her deeply.

'Yes . . . I don't know, maybe being pregnant does funny things to the brain.' She shrugged quickly, accepting the glass of wine that Yan poured and taking a rather hefty mouthful to bolster her nerves. 'But I . . . I'd been hesitating about telling you. I had no idea how you'd take it. We'd been together nearly all summer, but to be honest I just wasn't sure how you'd react to knowing I was pregnant . . .'

'As I said,' he murmured ruthlessly, 'you were in a romantic dream-world, Eleanor. You never made the effort to get to know me at all.'

'That's not fair, Yan . . .'

'It's the truth,' he persisted flatly. 'I filled the role as the legendary lover, maybe? In your storybook world? Then reality interfered. There's nothing more real than having a baby, is there, Eleanor? Giving life to a brand-new human being. That is the kind of thing which gives a relationship some deeper meaning, tests the honesty of the feelings involved. You were far too immature to handle any of that. So you snatched at whatever seemed the best line of defence, and ran away!'

'That is *so* unfair!' she breathed, shaking her head in miserable disbelief. 'How did you expect me to react, when Sofia and her parents came back from Italy and told me the truth?'

'As you were my fiancée, I *naïvely* expected you to give me the benefit of the doubt!'

She felt the colour surge to her face and then abruptly leave it.

'Yan, they were your *relatives*!' she said in a low voice. 'Your aunt, and her husband and step-daughter! They came to my lodgings, showed me Sofia's ring, and told me I'd been duped...'

There was a dangerous silence following this statement. The harsh lines of Yan's face seemed to be carved in bronze.

'And you couldn't wait to believe them,' he said at last, the deep voice clipped with suppressed fury. 'I had told you that Sofia and I were no longer engaged, that I broke off the engagement before you and I became involved, before she went on holiday to Italy...'

'Then *why* did Sofia lie?' Eleanor demanded huskily. 'Why did her parents—*your* aunt and uncle—lie?'

'Because they had a powerful desire to see me marry Sofia. To keep the family businesses "family". To close ranks, if you like, against threats from outside. They found it difficult to accept my true wishes.'

The cool explanation was offered without intonation. Yan revealed nothing of his emotions.

'You still spend a lot of time with Sofia,' she accused involuntarily, flinching as she saw the glitter of contempt in his gaze. 'If she was lying to me about your commitment to her, weren't you angry?'

'Yes, I was angry.' The wry note in his voice implied an understatement. 'But my stepcousin and

her family live here on the island. Family rifts can
be painful affairs. There is a limit to how long
grudges can be borne, Eleanor.'

'Sofia helps in the hotel. She was there for
breakfast that first morning, when I woke up in
your house. You and *Aunty* Sofia were planning
on taking Christophor out for the day! There's a
difference between forgiving and forgetting, and
actively seeking someone's company!'

'And jealousy is the most destructive emotion of
all,' he reminded her, with a glimmer of grim
amusement.

She stared at him in agitated silence. The food
arrived, and the distraction of eating had never
seemed more welcome.

They were arguing around in pointless circles, she
thought as she watched Yan take a calm mouthful
of his *dolmádhes*, bickering over how she could
have believed his aunt and Sofia, instead of him.
But the real issue wasn't whether or not he'd terminated his liaison with Sofia before proposing
marriage to Eleanor. It was his motives for proposing marriage. And, spin whatever fairy-tale explanation she could around that stark little scenario,
she found it quite impossible to believe that he'd
wanted to marry her for her own sake, that he'd
loved and cared enough for her to commit himself
to a lifelong relationship.

It had just been for the baby. He'd been dutiful—
admirably so. But love hadn't come into it . . . Was
she so wrong to have refused to settle for less?

'So you enjoyed helping out at the Thessa
Beach?' he enquired evenly. The mask was well and

truly back in place. If indeed it had ever slipped, she reflected bitterly.

'To be honest, yes!' She shot him a tight smile. 'It's been fun.'

'I have been considering developing health and fitness facilities,' he mused, leaning back in his chair and watching as she took a mouthful of roe salad with the delicious, fresh sesame bread. 'The water-sports angle is well catered for, naturally. The sea is right beside the hotel. But a gymnasium, a jacuzzi, perhaps hair and beauty treatments, perhaps even the novelty of your aromatherapy, might widen our appeal to guests from the mainland as well as from abroad.'

She gazed at him blankly, unsure where he was leading.

'There are probably just as many frazzled executives of both sexes in Athens as in London,' he added, eyeing her confusion with a flicker of laughter in his eyes.

'Yes ... I'm sure there would be,' she agreed cautiously. 'So ... ?'

'So I'd welcome your advice,' he finished up smoothly. 'You mentioned that you've been involved in building up similar lines at your aunt's hotel in England.'

'I ... yes.' She felt ridiculously flustered, annoyed at being thrown by this unexpected request. 'Yes, I did.' She shrugged slightly. 'And of course I'd be glad to offer any advice that I can.'

'*Efharisto*, Eleanor.' He smiled, wryly matching

her stiff formality. 'Do you have an example of the oils you use? In your aromatherapy remedies?'

'One or two.' She nodded, smiling at the waiter as her plate was whisked away and her main course put in its place. 'I always tend to travel with a lavender-based oil. It boosts the immune system— protects against infection...'

'Perhaps you should apply it to the rest of my staff at the hotel.' Yan grinned wickedly. 'To save me from any more staff shortages.'

She laughed uncertainly. 'Yes. Why not? Except that I doubt if I have sufficient quantities to treat your entire workforce!'

'Then perhaps, as the hotel owner, I should insist on a trial massage,' he followed up calmly, a gleam in his eyes. 'Come to my room tonight; see if you can convince me of its therapeutic merits, Eleanor.'

She stared at him, resenting his mockery, his cool certainty that she'd shy away from such a challenge.

'Fine.' She shrugged carelessly, clenching her fists in her lap to hide their sudden trembling. 'If that's what you want...'

The dark gaze had narrowed derisively on her flushed face. Anger sparkling in her eyes, she levelled a direct glare across the candlelit table at him.

'You needn't look at me like that, Yan!' she said frostily. 'I told you, there's nothing remotely... sensual about the kind of massage I do...!'

He held her gaze, his own expression altering to one of elaborate gravity.

'I believe you, little one. I shall greatly look forward to this extraordinarily unsensual massage.

Meanwhile——' he watched the colour changes in her face as she fought to control her temper '—shall we finish our meal and go to watch some dancing?'

CHAPTER SEVEN

THE dancing was already well under way by the time they arrived. Tucked into the side of the mountain, the Theopolou taverna was tremendously popular with tourists and Greeks alike. Not even the invading mosquitos could keep the crowds away. Chunks of some special kind of mosquito repellent were kept burning all night, in small metal braziers near the low parapet overlooking the mountainside and the distant sea. Far away down at the sea, tiny spangles of light dotted the darkness. Up here, the red-checked tables were full of people finishing meals and drinking wine, retsina, coffee or liqueurs. A buzz of laughter and excitement filled the air. And on the small dance-floor three people— a man and two lissom girls—were performing classic folk dances to live bouzouki music.

Yan's uncle—Sofia's father—waved through the crowd and came over as they arrived. A short, swarthy-skinned man in his late fifties, with a drooping moustache, he was island born and bred, and intensely proud of it.

'Yan! And Eleanor!' He beamed, as if the gap in their acquaintance had been four weeks, not four years. 'Welcome! Welcome to my taverna, Eleanor! How lovely to meet you again!' He pumped her hand enthusiastically.

'Thank you. You too. I ... I hope your wife is well.'

'Quite well, thank you. My little girl Sofia is here; have you seen her yet, Yan?'

Eleanor stiffened. Yan's arm, which had been slung proprietorially around her shoulders in a way which aroused conflicting emotions, tightened imperceptibly.

'Not yet. Can we have a bottle of your best white wine at the table over there, Stefan?'

'No problem. When I find Sofia I will send her over, *ne*?'

Was the man deliberately stirring up trouble, Eleanor wondered bitterly, or was he just naturally thick-skinned with a very short memory?

'Just the wine will do, Stefan,' Yan advised, a harder trace of grim amusement in his voice.

Still smiling, the other man nodded, then hesitated before turning to go. '*Endaxi*, just the wine. But tell me, Eleanor, how is your beautiful little son, Christophor?'

'He's fine,' she said woodenly, forcing a smile. 'He's safely in bed, with Evangelie in charge.'

'Such a bright, intelligent child,' Uncle Stefan enthused, without the slightest embarrassment. 'When Yan brought him back to Skiathos we were all instantly captivated, Eleanor.'

'I'm so glad.' The polite reply tripped off her tongue, meaningless and inane.

'I suppose you'll be staying until Christophor's Name Day,' Stefan persisted blithely. 'The first week in August.'

'I... I'm not sure...' She was going to scream, she thought hysterically. This double-edged, ambiguous conversation was the worst she'd endured. Did he mean were she and Christophor staying that long? Or was he implying that Christophor would be staying anyway, and that she undoubtedly would be going home alone?

'The wine, Uncle Stefan?' The grim note was there, the amusement now fast fading in Yan's clipped, incisive tone.

Eleanor followed Yan through the throngs to a table in a quiet corner of the taverna, near the parapet with its dizzy view down the dark mountainside. The candles were shaded in smoky glass globes. The rough white-painted walls and bamboo roof were hung with vines and creepers.

Yan glanced at her obliquely as they sat down. 'You remember the Skiathan emphasis on Name Days?'

'Of course. I'd... I'd forgotten that "Christophoros" was celebrated in early August...'

'The sixth of August this year. The day of the Transfiguration.'

She nodded, her brain racing. She'd experienced several 'Name Days', and loved the atmosphere. Name Days in Greece were rather like one huge, communal birthday party, but given if anything rather more prominence than actual birthdays. Whenever someone's name coincided with a Saint's Day, or a major day in the Greek Orthodox calendar, a party was held in that person's honour. And in Skiathos, each person in the town or village with that name held open house, their doors flung wide to all-comers, home-made liqueurs and sweet home-made pastries called *hamalia*, with almonds, honey, cinnamon and breadcrumbs, ready for visitors flocking to bring small gifts and to wish the celebrant '*Chronia Polla*'...

'The relatives will expect Christophor to be here?' she managed at last, non-committally.

'Naturally. So will I, Eleanor.'

She regarded him in silence, struggling with conflicting emotions. Maybe her own feelings of antagonism were irrelevant, when something as important as this concerned Christophor. He was too small to choose. But did she have any right to deprive Yan's son of such a rich, uniquely Greek experience, something that was part of his natural heritage?

She needed a little time to think...

The night air was alive with the singing of crickets, and redolent with the thick aroma of cooling pine needles. From over by the huge charcoal cooking fires wafted the mouth-watering aroma of spit-roasting pork and chicken. She'd been here many times with Yan, that long-ago summer when they'd been together. Little had changed. Only Uncle Stefan's topics of conversation...

'The dancers are good,' she commented lightly, switching subjects, twisting round in her seat to watch them. 'I adore Greek dancing. I adore bouzouki, too. It's one of the most joyful sounds I've ever heard!'

'I remember.' Yan was watching her beneath lidded eyes, his expression unfathomable.

'Do you?' She glanced at him, with a half-smile. 'Is that why you brought me here again? Because I enjoyed it so much in the past?'

'Why else would I subject you to Uncle Stefan's rhinoceros hide?' His expression was ironic.

'Your uncle was charming,' she pointed out cautiously. The crooked twist of Yan's mouth spoke such volumes of his wry sense of humour, his ability to see the comical side of even the direst of situations... Was it the modest amount of alcohol she'd consumed so far tonight, or was she actually beginning to find Yan's company as warmly compulsive as she had in the past?

The wine was delivered in a silver ice-bucket by a smiling waiter.

'Are you still hungry?' Yan murmured, inspecting the label and indicating cool approval. 'Or can I merely tempt you to some of this wine? It was made in a monastery in the mountains near Thessaloniki, on the mainland. It's quite pleasant.'

'I couldn't eat another thing, even though that pork smells wonderful,' she confessed. 'I'll settle for the wine.'

'The night is young.' Yan's wry comment jolted her back to the past. They'd laughed over this particular phrase together, had similar conversations, said similar things so often that she'd lost count. 'We could eat again later. Take in another club, if you like.'

She met Yan's eyes, smiling involuntarily. Then the laughter faded, and his eyes, lazily lidded, moved slowly down over the low-cut, shoe-string-strapped bodice, where the full globes of her breasts were visibly outlined beneath the pink silk. Her throat dried. She fought down stubborn, idiotic waves of warmth, insidious ripples of answering desire.

'You look beautiful, Eleanor,' he said softly. There was a light in the depths of his eyes which seemed to touch her, made her tingle all over.

She was desperately searching her brain for the right words to say, when she glimpsed someone all too familiar through the crowds.

Sofia. Like the proverbial bad penny.

Her heart contracting, she watched the Greek girl heading for their table. There was a smile of barely concealed malice on her brightly painted mouth. In a clinging stretch-tapestry mini-dress, outlining every curve of her body, high-heeled gold shoes and her riotous black curls loose in a cloud around her shoulders, she looked so outrageously vampish and glamorous that Eleanor immediately felt gauche and unfashionable.

'Yan!' The husky voice throbbed with pleasure. She bent to kiss him on the cheek, with barely a glance at Eleanor. 'Darling, I'm surprised to see you here. Weren't you planning on getting an early night?'

'Hello, Sofia.' Yan's greeting held just a hint of cool steel.

'Goodness, Sofia,' Eleanor heard herself saying mildly, 'you do get around! Everywhere I go, there you are!'

The barbed remark drew the other girl's grey glare.

'Not quite everywhere you go, Eleanor.' She smiled, her voice deceptively light. 'I didn't see you in *Athens*, for example.'

It took several seconds for the full implications of this calm statement to sink in. And then, with a thunderbolt of understanding, Eleanor closed her eyes tightly on the dark wash of pain, and realised how relatively relaxed and happy she'd been feeling over the last few minutes. Dangerously relaxed and happy...

Thank heavens for Sofia Theopolou, she reflected with a shaft of black humour. If she hadn't marched up and dragged things back to full, sordid reality, there might have been an outside chance of making a complete fool of herself all over again tonight...

Standing up, she found that her legs were trembling uncontrollably. She willed herself to stay calm.

'I wouldn't want to deprive you of that early night, Yan,' she said, her voice jerky, quite unlike her own. 'Maybe you'd like to share it with Sofia? I'll get a taxi back...'

She pushed past the Greek girl, attempting to make as dignified an exit as possible, not an easy feat with tears blurring her eyes. Before she'd managed it, Yan had risen to his full height, catching her arm and pinioning her to the spot. There was a frightening blaze of anger in his dark eyes. But this time it was directed at Sofia.

'Enough,' he breathed harshly. 'I have a rule never to hit a woman. But tonight, Sofia, I am tempted to break my rule...'

The softly contemptuous-sounding exchange of Greek which followed was too fast for Eleanor to understand. She stood mutinously, Yan's fierce grip digging painfully into her upper arm, too proud to writhe and fight.

'I'll take you home.' He cast a brief, bleak glance over her hostile face, and then turned to lead her from the taverna, leaving Sofia standing by their table, her expression unreadable.

'There's really no need,' she began, with icy politeness, as he propelled her towards the jeep. 'I'm sure Uncle Stefan would be *delighted* to ring for a taxi to get me out of the way.'

'Will you shut up?' The imperious hiss of his words made her flinch slightly, despite her own burning anger.

She sat in seething silence as they drove back down the mountain. The barely controlled savagery of his acceleration and gear changes left her in no doubt about Yan's similar mood.

Nearing his house, she found her voice again.

'I hope you're not still expecting the trial aromatherapy massage tonight.' She'd intended the comment to be sweetly sarcastic. Instead it came out husky, unsteady.

Yan ground the jeep to a halt on the dark drive outside the house, switched off the ignition, jumped out, and came around to take her arm.

'Will you believe me if I swear to you that I did not take Sofia to Athens with me?' he ground out impatiently.

'Going on past experience?' she goaded shakily. 'Frankly, no...'

'That,' he rapped out peremptorily, 'is exactly what I thought you'd say!' His hold on her arm tightened unbearably.

'Are you going to apply matching bruises to this side?' she queried acidly as his grip bit into her flesh. 'I'd just like to know why tonight's revelations appear to be *my* fault. Sofia let your sordid little secret slip. Why stop the circulation in *my* arms?'

The curse torn from Yan's lips was in roughly guttural Greek, and was doubtless unrepeatable. Twisting her abruptly into his arms, he silenced her with a kiss of such suppressed violence that Eleanor felt an answering shudder rock her body. Hardly aware of what was happening, she found herself partially released while he reached for something in the rear of the jeep, and then swept into his arms to be carried, bodily, away from the silent house, through the gardens and down on to the empty curve of his private beach. The white launch rocked on the dark water, eerie in the brilliant moonlight.

'Yan, what the hell are you doing...?' she whispered, tense as a reed as she writhed in his arms. He flung a large dark blue rug to the white sand, in the shadow of a group of pines.

'I am doing what I should have done the moment you arrived in Skiathos, Eleanor,' he bit out jerkily, thrusting her flat on the rug and catching the thick swath of brown hair to pin her down as she tried in outrage to wriggle back up. 'With you, talking is useless. It's time to demonstrate my feelings in the only goddamned way you seem to understand...'

Trapped beneath his long, muscular weight, abruptly besieged by the onslaught of subtle, expert caresses as he explored her body through the thin covering of clothes, Eleanor felt a raw fury she'd never known before. Lovemaking should be by consent, not force, shouldn't it? How dared Yan Diamakis think he could switch attention from his trip to Athens by physically subduing her?

The hot, indignant, savage protests whirled around in her brain as his raid on her senses continued. The point at which her wild fury transmuted to desire was blurred and hazy. But one minute she was rigid with distaste, the next she was convulsed in a breathless rage of sensual awareness.

'Yan, please . . . oh, please . . .' She hardly knew her own voice.

'Please what?' The throaty taunt was breathed against the soft swell of her breasts as his insistent hands moulded and cupped, and his mouth sucked and nipped at her taut nipples through the wet pink silk. 'Please do this? Or perhaps this? Oh, yes, sweet Eleanor, be patient . . .' The thick, triumphant purr brought a red haze of fury and desire, confusingly mingled, swamping her defences, scrambling rational argument.

Flattened on the rug, she felt him lever his leg between her tightly clenched knees, separating her legs, forcing submission. Eyes closed, emotions ragged, she shivered with a thrill of convulsive hunger as the silk dress was thrust unceremoniously higher, the smooth length of her thighs exposed to his shadowed gaze.

'It's a hunter's moon,' Yan grated softly, sliding strong, possessive fingers all the way up her legs, tantalisingly continuing up over her flat, hotly melting stomach, slipping the thin straps of her bodice down to slither the dress free of her arching breasts, naked beneath the soft silk. 'So I can see to make love to my fierce little captive. You are enchanting in moonlight, *agapití mou*. You take my breath away...'

'Oh, Yan...!' His whispered words were raggedly humorous, but thick with carnal knowledge. Her low sob was half reproach, half moan of desire.

His mouth dropped to lick the tip of one tense nipple, and she gasped involuntarily as flames of reaction heated her whole body.

'Do you like that?' He was softly savage, moving his tongue to the other tight peak, then gathering both swollen globes hard against his lips as she shuddered and writhed, helplessly aroused.

'Yes...oh, yes...!' Even as she moaned the surrender, she hated herself, she dimly registered, but the force of attraction was too overwhelming, the chemistry too explosive. She was too dizzy with need to lie passive any longer. She wanted to stroke and explore his hard body, to give pleasure as well as receive it. The gloriously male planes and hollows, some hair-roughened, some like silken steel, were agonisingly familiar, and with a choked sob she let her fingers begin a sensory investigation of their own.

In a turmoil of impatience, she found herself stripped naked in the moonlight, with Yan's shirt and trousers flung off with haphazard lack of aim to join her discarded clothes on the sand. With his lips and fingers he kissed and caressed, finally circling decisively around the secret warm, slick moistness which told him exactly how much she wanted him . . .

'You're exquisite,' he breathed raggedly, bending his head to trail kisses of fire along the quivering plane of her stomach, spreading her widely with gentle forcefulness to gaze at the moon-silvered prize of her body, 'like a flower, sweet Eleanor, moist with dew . . .'

'Yan . . . !' She choked his name in a wild paroxysm of impatience, reaching with fierce shyness to pull him down to her, trembling from head to toe, taut as piano wire as passion flooded her whole being. 'Don't stop now, don't you *dare* stop now, or I swear I *will* kill you . . . !'

'Then I shall preserve my life, little savage,' he assured her thickly, taking her breath away by plunging victoriously inside her. The triumphant possession was accomplished with such stretching, invading completeness that Eleanor cried out in utter abandon, her gasped, agonised exclamation echoing round the moonlit beach. The wonder of finally giving herself to Yan, after so long, was like a blaze of light, white-hot, brilliant. Nothing could ever match this intensity of feeling, she thought feverishly. Nothing in the normal ebb and flow of daily existence could even come close to matching it . . .

The helpless waves of sizzling pleasure mounted rhythmically, higher and higher, until the relentless surge, the wild, frantic explosion, the splintering of her senses into a rush of frenzied release which threatened to drown her in dense, dangerous amnesia...

Amnesia lasted no longer than ten minutes, while they lay closely entwined in the silence. Gradually, sense began to creep back. The silence wasn't silence: it was the soft wash of the sea on the beach a few yards away; it was the high, monotonous shrilling of the crickets in the dry scrub and the pine trees all around them. Levering herself up on her elbows, she tensed, pulled herself free. His face was shadowy, unreadable in the moonlight. He looked like a stranger again. She hated herself, and she hated him...

'So now, just through physical possession, I understand your feelings?' she hazarded huskily, on a soft, choked laugh. 'Don't you know how small that makes me feel, Yan?'

'Small?' His deep voice was still rough, his breathing still harsh. 'Dealing with you is like skirting a quicksand, Eleanor. At least I've established one solid fact. You still want me every bit as urgently as I still want you.'

'But can't you see?' Tears were stinging her eyes. She was glad of the darkness. She didn't want him to see her crying. 'Yan, resorting to sex is just...just brushing the rest under the carpet. Just because you can make me want you, doesn't mean you can make me trust you...'

With a hoarse, self-mocking groan, he rolled abruptly on to his stomach, dropped his forehead on to his forearms.

Eleanor found that she'd curled herself up into as small an area as possible, her arms clutched around her legs as she fought down the misery beginning to engulf her again.

'Sofia is trying to cause trouble again,' he said slowly, raising his head to level an intent gaze on Eleanor's white face. 'Short of locking her in her own house, I doubt if I can stop her from malicious meddling until you have finally agreed to marry me, Eleanor. Does that make sense to you?'

She was silent now, her throat tight. An impossible yearning was tearing at her heart, a desperate need to believe him. If only she could feel secure in the knowledge that he was proposing marriage because he loved her, not because she was the mother of his son...

'Sofia knows that because you are not Greek, because you are unsure and vulnerable and insecure in a foreign land, she has the perfect victim for her little games,' Yan went on bleakly, a humourless smile on his mouth. 'Surely, Eleanor, the fact that I have not married Sofia during this last four years tells you *something*?'

'But if Sofia had got herself pregnant?' Eleanor whispered, forcing herself to say the words. 'Would you have married her, Yan?'

'What kind of a damn fool question is that?' he demanded incredulously, levering himself up to stare into her eyes.

'*Would* you?'

'That situation would not have arisen.' The words were drily mocking.

'But if she had, of course you would have offered to marry her,' Eleanor persisted angrily.

'I fail to see what you are trying to prove,
Eleanor.'

'That . . . that it's your *child* you care about. Not
me. And maybe not Sofia either. But certainly not
me . . .'

As Yan slowly shook his head, his dark face
deadpan, she was scrambling shakily to her feet.
She grabbed her dress and flung it over her head,
snatching up the small pair of silk knickers that
she'd discarded along with her shoes, and then she
was walking, half running, up the beach towards
the house.

Yan didn't follow her. In trembling silence, she
showered, and then climbed miserably into bed. But
she didn't relax until she finally heard the jeep being
gunned into life and roaring away. Where had he
gone? Back to his apartment at the hotel? Or back
up to the taverna, maybe? To have a passionate row
with Sofia? And how would that end? Eleanor
wondered with bitter cynicism. What a short-sighted
fool Sofia was. All these years longing to be Yan's
wife. And all she had to do was become pregnant,
and her goal would be achieved . . .

Hot tears came at last. Part of her brain—the
rational part—accepted that this argument was
ramshackle and totally lacking in logic. But the pain
of giving herself to Yan, of knowing how deeply
she loved him, but receiving no words of love in
return, had cut too deep for logic. He didn't love
her. He despised her. Look at his taunts earlier, at
the beach bar. How she was 'lacking a track record

of honesty'. Anything more coldly contemptuous
would be hard to imagine...

Tonight's brief, insidious moments of rapport
had been fatally seductive. It was tempting to con-
strue their explosion of passion on the beach as a
sign that all was well between them. But the truth
was, they didn't trust each other. The scars of the
past couldn't be healed. She was wasting her time
longing for them to be...

As the small hours crept past, and she tossed and
turned in her bed, she realised that her only course
of action was to get away. She had to get away. She
had to have time to think, away from Yan, away
from the tension and pressure of his overwhelming
demands, his potent presence...

She crept out of bed, and began to pack her
suitcase, collecting Christophor's few—mainly
new—possessions as he slept. As late as she dared
leave it, she gently woke him and carried him
downstairs, whispering to him to stay quiet. In the
safety of the kitchen, she sat him down with urgent
instructions for quiet, and a biscuit and a drink of
fruit juice, while she tiptoed back up for her
suitcase. The taxi firm in Skiathos thankfully
seemed to operate an all-night service. She gave
them a pick-up point about a quarter of a mile along
the road, well away from the house, or the hotel.
Then, feeling like a thief in the night, she stole out
of the house in the early dawn and started walking,
holding her son's small hand as tightly as she could.

'It's an adventure game.' She smiled, stopping
for a few seconds to ease the weight of the suitcase,
and pressing her finger warningly to her lips. 'We

have to see how quiet we can be, so we don't wake anyone up.'

Christophor, large, trusting dark eyes solemnly meeting hers, nodded in agreement. Together they slowly rounded the end of the drive, and joined the main road. From there it was just a case of keeping going, of trying to control the violent thudding of her heart, the shivers of fear coursing through her. She felt like a refugee, fleeing from oppression. The whimsical thought made her smile. Yan might be many things, but he could hardly be lumped in the same category as a tyrant of war, threatening her life...

At the airport she finally breathed a sigh of relief. This far, and surely nothing could go wrong. All she needed was a flight, two seats to anywhere. She'd already resolved to accept whatever was available to any European destination, within reason. From there she could transfer to another flight and get back to England. This sense of urgency was increasing with every minute that passed, as if not only Yan, and his meddlesome relatives, but the entire island were conspiring to trap her here, or to take her child away from her...

'We have seats available on a flight to Rome, due to leave in around forty minutes,' the young male desk clerk informed her, putting down his telephone and staring at a computer screen. 'Will you take those?'

'Yes.' The wave of relief strengthened. Forty minutes was nothing. She and Christophor could buy a drink in the small cafeteria, and she could keep him amused by continuing the adventure story, making it all seem like one big game.

Tickets in her hand, she checked in her suitcase, with a sense of finality, and went in search of drinks and recreation. The flight was called a little earlier than expected. Lifting Christophor into her arms, she made her way with a group of other passengers towards the barrier.

'Passport?' The burly man waited impassively as Eleanor dug into her hand luggage and located the wallet containing all her important papers. Slipping her fingers inside it, she fumbled and searched. Bewildered realisation dawned like a blow to her stomach, a physical sinking sensation. She went hot and cold in panic and embarrassment.

'Passport!' There was impatience and boredom in equal measures in the man's voice. The queue behind her was shuffling curiously to observe the outcome. Scarlet in the face, wishing the floor would open and swallow her, she shook her head.

'I'm sorry,' she managed, with a choked, despairing groan, 'I'm afraid that I . . . I don't seem to have my passport with me.'

CHAPTER EIGHT

THE moment she saw Yan, waiting calmly in the
jeep outside the airport, the truth hit her. Yan. It
must have been him. *Yan* had gone through her
things, taken her passport, effectively *imprisoning*
her here in Skiathos...

The fury erupted like a furnace inside her. The
arrogance, the sheer cold-blooded tyranny of the
man...

When he saw her, he jumped down and came to
meet them. He was tall and deadpan, in jeans and
denim shirt, thick black hair windblown from the
drive. To his dubious credit, he refrained from actually gloating. His face was devoid of expression
as he bent to gather an increasingly fractious
Christophor into his arms, and took the case from
Eleanor's clenched fingers.

'Papa!' Christophor was exclaiming in delight,
his attack of the whines forgotten, putting his arms
around Yan's neck in a surge of happiness.
'Mummy and me were having a 'venture. Is the
'venture over now?'

'Just temporarily postponed, poppet,' Eleanor
said through her teeth. 'Mummy lost something we
needed for the adventure.'

'Did you mislay something?' Yan queried, deeply
ironic. The narrowed gaze scanned her dishevelled
appearance—navy culottes and blouse grabbed in

143

haste, her hair dragged into a speedy ponytail. Christophor, resplendent in his new Greek bermudas and T-shirt, thrust his thumb firmly into his mouth and fell silent, dark eyes wide and watchful as he absorbed some of the tense adult vibrations.

She drew a long, shaky breath before she even dared speak to Yan.

'Yes. As a matter of fact,' she responded in a saccharine voice, 'I found that I'd mislaid my passport.'

'Ah. I believe I may have the answer to that.'

Not the faintest *trace* of repentance in the deep drawl. She climbed stiffly into the back of the jeep, and took Christophor on to her lap.

'I'm sure you have,' she murmured, bitterly sarcastic. 'So what happens now? Am I thrown into your dungeon, tortured on the rack?'

'Nothing so extreme has been planned so far,' Yan admitted, with a wry glance back over his shoulder as he drove out of the airport. 'Maybe what happens now is that you face the simple truth, Eleanor.'

'Oh? And what might that be?'

'That I want you to stay. That I would do almost anything to stop you from leaving here. And that, deep in your heart, you want to say.'

'Do I?' She could hardly believe her ears. 'So why do you think I was about to board the next flight out of here?'

'Because you are afraid to face the truth.'

She was seethingly silent as this cool statement blew in the wind around her.

'What an extraordinary conversation this is,' she managed at last. 'Is this *another* truth we're talking about now? This "truth" you say I am afraid to face?'

'Yes, I believe it is.' Yan's shoulders looked very broad and powerful, the muscles evident beneath the denim as he drove. She stared with burning anger at this proud, heartless back. 'I think you are afraid to face the fact that you love me.'

She found herself stunned and speechless at this flagrant piece of arrogance. Hugging Christophor tightly in her arms, she fought down waves of heat. Resentment churned inside her. She was to face the fact that *she* loved *him*? Not that *he* loved *her*! Of all the patronising, manipulative, diabolical . . .

Never, *never* would she admit again that she loved him. She must be demented to love him, she flayed herself silently. How could any sane, practical European female love such a . . . a barbarian, such a desperado—satisfyingly excruciating insults briefly failed her—such a *man*?

Evangelie, clearly distraught to find their possessions gone, the house empty on waking, greeted the return of Christophor with such a demonstration of tearful relief that Eleanor found herself actually feeling mean and small at her attempt at deception. She firmly clamped down on the idiotic feeling. She was a free British citizen; she had every right to be allowed to take her small son and go home if she damn well pleased . . .

'You had a telephone call while you were gone,' the housekeeper informed Eleanor, a reproachful light in her eyes which cast yet more guilt on

Eleanor's shoulders. 'Your friend Geoffrey Terence-Evans.'

Yan's dark face hardened into the familiar mocking mask.

'So you hadn't told this "Geoffrey" what you were planning?' he queried softly, following her on to the terrace and down into the garden while Evangelie occupied herself with Christophor. There was a carved wooden bench beneath a gnarled, ancient olive tree. Suddenly exhausted, Eleanor sat down on it heavily. Above her the delicate silvery leaves hid hundreds of small, slowly ripening olives, greeny-grey fruits. She thought of how, when all the holiday-makers had gone, in the chilly winter months, the island people gathered these small fruits by hand from scores of olive groves, an extraordinarily time-consuming labour of love...

'Well? Had you, Eleanor?'

She couldn't look at Yan. Instead she fixed her mutinous gaze on the sunlit Aegean, flashing sparks of sapphire between the trees and flowers.

'No. It was rather a spur-of-the-moment idea.'

Yan sat down on the bench, uncomfortably close. The shimmer of suppressed anger seemed to vibrate physically between them, like invisible barbs of wire.

'Because of what we did on the beach last night?' he hazarded softly. The rough timbre in his voice made her stomach contract in an abrupt rush of memory.

'Because of...everything! Because of you, Sofia——'

'*Forget* Sofia.'

'All right, even if I could forget Sofia, that still leaves Christophor . . . !'

'But you love Christophor.'

'Of course I do!'

'Yet you don't want what is best for him?'

Swinging round to face him, she felt all the pain and frustration of the last few days erupt in a surge of bitter fury.

'I'm his mother! Don't you dare tell me what you think is best for him! My getting pregnant four years ago was an unfortunate accident. The only reason I told you about Christophor was because . . . because I didn't want him to hate me for keeping his real father away from him, like *my* mother did to me . . .'

There was a taut silence as Yan stared at her white face.

'Is that what happened, Eleanor? Your mother lied to you about your father?'

'Yes . . . I discovered it when she died. I found letters. My father had wanted to see me. But he'd left her for another woman, and she was too bitter to let him near me . . .' It still hurt, she thought dimly. Even after all this time. That deprivation still cut deep . . .

'Eleanor——' Yan's deep voice was harsh '—is *that* why you wouldn't marry me? The real reason?' He caught her chin, twisting her round. 'Because you imagined history might repeat itself? That I'd walk out on you and the baby?'

'Face it, with the deception over Sofia, you weren't a particularly good bet at the time!'

'You think I would walk out, abandon my own *son*?'

She glared at him, shaking all over as he stared into her eyes.

'Who knows?' she shot at him bitterly. 'Anyway, no matter *what* you feel about having a son, Yan, it doesn't give you the right to act like a ... a damn dictator, ruling my life, forbidding me to leave, hiding my passport! I can't believe you did that! I just can't believe it! If I'd ever feared you were possessive, autocratic, some ... some throw-back to the nineteenth century who'd lock me up under the thumb of his family and throw away the key, this morning proves me right!'

There was a towering silence. Then her heart contracted painfully as he leaned across to cup her face in his hands, bent his head to cover her lips with his own. His kiss was ruthlessly gentle, cruelly coaxing. Last night's abandon rushed back through her like molten lava. But her fury over this morning's fiasco gave her the strength to resist him, to clench her jaw, her teeth, her whole body, to fend off this treacherous invasion of her senses.

He lifted his head, and she saw a wry gleam of bleak humour in his eyes. Slowly he traced a thumb over the full, swollen curve of her lower lip, circled both thumbs over her stubbornly set jawline, and up to the high jut of her cheekbones. His touch was fatally intimate. Every nerve-ending seemed to scream silently for more.

'So frozen and lifeless. Like poor Daphne and her bay-tree. Terrified of that wicked, lecherous god Apollo. And yet last night we had more than sex together, Eleanor. We made love, the most powerful love I've ever experienced. I needed to feel your response to me, to tell me what I wanted to know. So tell me now, to my face, that you don't love me.'

It was diabolical, she reflected, dimly hanging on to her beleaguered defences. He was a monster. How dared he use last night as a cunning lever to get what he wanted now?

'Tell me,' he persisted roughly. 'I want to hear you say the words.'

'You want to hear me say that I love you?' she choked hoarsely. 'You can go to *hell*, Yan. I *don't* love you! I *loathe* you. Do you hear me? I *detest* you! You're a fool . . . you're completely deranged if you think I'll ever marry you!'

He released her slowly, and they stared at each other, eyes locked in a tense clash of brilliant sea-green and unreadable black. Her torrent of abuse seemed to have fallen on coolly shuttered ears, from the implacable stillness on Yan's face. But when he finally spoke, she felt a faint jolt of surprise.

'All right.' He gave a jerky nod, and thrust a lean hand through his dark hair, flexing powerful shoulders as if to ease the build-up of tension. Her throat drying, she found she couldn't take her eyes away from his taut face. All right? What did he mean by 'all right'? Finally, he seemed to have his emotions under control. He twisted a harsh, bleak smile, which somehow didn't quite reach his eyes.

'All right . . .' he said again, more forcefully. 'You win. You can go back to England with Christophor. But only if you stay until the sixth of August. If you stay until the celebrations for Christophor's Name Day.'

She stared at him in blank confusion. Was he really saying it? Offering complete freedom, as long as she stayed for the party?

'Do you swear, on your honour, that I'll be free to go with Christophor?' she demanded, her voice husky.

'On those terms. Yes. I swear, on my honour, Eleanor, that you will be free to go with Christophor.' The deep voice sounded slightly raw. He was telling the truth, she realised. Nothing else would roughen his voice with that suppressed pain and anger...

She turned away, fighting back tears. Idiotic tears. Foolish, weak and pathetic. She'd won. This was her victory. Why should Yan's pain transmit itself to her? Why should she feel this contraction of matching pain inside herself? Hadn't he caused her more than her fair share of pain in the past? Wasn't he causing it again now?

With an effort, she hardened her heart. Maybe her victory had a painfully hollow feel about it, but it was the only option, her only escape route.

'I agree, then,' she said in a muffled voice, head turned away. 'I'll stay until the celebrations. Then I'll go.'

'One other condition,' Yan said shortly.

Her heart plummeted. Swinging round, she found the dark gaze gleaming with an unreadable expression which triggered fresh tremors of uneasiness.

'What?'

'Don't look so suspicious.' His tone was drily ironic. 'I would be deeply grateful, Eleanor, if you would continue to help out in the hotel, and to advise on the plans we discussed last night.'

The relief felt intense. 'Is that all? Of course. It will help to pass the time,' she retorted blandly. She found that she was surreptitiously crossing her fingers behind her back. Was this how prisoners felt, presented with the prospect of imminent parole? Quite how she'd cope with her freedom, when it came, was a hurdle she'd cross when she had to. Freedom from Yan was a bittersweet prospect...

'*Efharisto*, Eleanor,' Yan murmured, standing up. 'And I trust,' he added, with softly mocking formality, 'that your remaining time here will pass as quickly as you would wish it to.'

Her vision of time passing slowly was proved right, she realised, but not for the reasons she'd implied. Had Yan known exactly how it would be when he forced her to agree to his conditions?

Had he fiendishly foreseen the unbearable sensual tension which would build up, even more unbearable than before?

He didn't touch her again after their fraught agreement in the garden. But to her chagrin, she found that he didn't need to. Every look, every mocking glance, every time the hateful man stood just that fraction too close for her nerves to bear, she trembled like jelly. Her skin feathered with goose-bumps. Her heart started thudding too fast,

and her knees went weak. What on earth was wrong
with her?

To make matters ten times worse, as well as Yan's
insistence that she help out again at the hotel, she
was forced to endure what transpired to be com-
pulsory water-skiing sessions, outings, riding,
swimming, boat trips and picnics on remote
northern beaches and meals with Yan and
Christophor, so that, presumably, he could spend
as much time with his small son as possible before
he left. During these sessions, Eleanor had expected Yan to be caustic and accusing in his at-
titude towards her. Instead, he appeared as usual:
cool, slightly unfathomable, wryly humorous. In
short, dangerously, unnervingly good company. She
had no idea what was really going on in his head.
If she'd thought he'd be childishly sulking over her
refusal to stay, she had to acknowledge reluctantly
that he had a great deal more maturity.

But from the previous relentlessly physical onslaught, Yan had switched, apparently without
effort, to an almost priest-like restraint. By the eve
of Christophor's party, she was absolutely mor-
tified to admit to herself that she was a shivering
wreck of suppressed longing.

'I am in London quite regularly,' Yan informed
her briefly, after they'd spent an hour water-skiing
and walked the short distance up the beach to have
coffee at the beach bar. 'On business. I would like
to visit Christophor whenever I am in England.'

'I . . . yes, of course.' Business in London? Was
this another catch?

Sitting in swimsuit and damp T-shirt, with Yan gloriously lean and male and disturbing in similar attire, she was tingling all over with the contemptible urge to reach out and touch him. She'd never forgive him for this, she thought darkly, swirling the milk around in her coffee with a jerky twist of the spoon and watching the pale blend with dark in a spiral of contrasts. Subjecting her to this extra week of his company, making her die inside from wanting him and hating him...

'Why haven't you mentioned this before?' she felt compelled to ask.

'It wasn't relevant.'

'Wasn't *relevant*? Oh, no. I see. You weren't going to mention it until you'd given up hope of trapping me here in Greece?'

'This "trapped" theme of yours is becoming tedious,' he countered, his voice hardening. 'You speak as if I were some blinkered, narrow-minded despot, with no conception of a world beyond my own country. Why should it surprise you to learn that I regularly travel the world, Eleanor? That I might, in fact, be an enlightened, relatively civilised human being?'

She managed a sweetly sarcastic raise of the eyebrows.

'Well, now, I wonder, why *should* that surprise me?' she goaded lightly. Her dubious reward was the narrowing of Yan's dark eyes, and the answering gleam.

'Do not push me, Eleanor. I have behaved with exemplary self-control...'

'Though you say so yourself,' she agreed mockingly.

'Modest to a fault.' He grinned faintly, unperturbed. 'And that self-control is my armour against your insults, sweet Eleanor. How else do you imagine I have endured your foolish accusations?'

'Can you be more specific?'

'That I would have married you, then walked out and abandoned you for another woman. Or, perhaps even worse, locked you up, subjected you to limited freedom under the chaperonage of my family,' he bit out coolly. 'Have you forgotten that my mother was as English as you are? That my parents' marriage was happy? That, far from being under lock and key, my mother lived a surprisingly *normal* life? Do you have any idea how it makes me feel to know that you could even half believe such nonsense?'

Eleanor felt her cheeks warming under his scathing gaze.

'Sofia said . . .' she began, then stopped abruptly, recalling another, similar conversation with Yan, and his derisive response. 'Laura warned me that things would be very different from England,' she added crisply. 'And look at the way you've behaved with my passport.'

The dark gaze lidded a fraction more, effectively veiling his thoughts.

'Taking your passport was merely my insurance against your habit of running away from situations without using your brain.'

'You see? You're totally unrepentant. And you insult me into the bargain!'

She got up, quivering with suppressed emotion. 'I'm going back to see if I can help Evangelie with some of her baking for tomorrow...'

'Don't forget to make sure that your suitcase is packed again,' Yan advised tauntingly. 'Tomorrow you have your much longed-for freedom, Eleanor.'

Her throat tight, she forced a smile, spinning on her heel in the sand as she turned to walk away.

'Did you imagine for one moment that I'd forgotten?' she flung back over her shoulder, wishing that her heart would stop its fierce, stubborn aching, irrespective of the calm logic of her brain...

'Eleanor! My dear...!' Alexandros Diamakis, Yan's father, detached himself from the mêlée of guests and family to come with outstretched hands to speak to her. 'I cannot tell you how good it is to see you here in Skiathos again!' he said as he kissed her cheek. 'Your glass is empty. Let me get you another.' He drew her away from the others, across to a table laden with drinks.

'It's lovely to see you again.' She smiled at him, the bleak feeling inside deepening. The Name Day party was in full swing, had been nearly all day. Tonight, though, a live band had been hired, and the haunting strains of Greek folk music were being played on bouzouki, guitar and violin. Trays of food, including the *mezedhakia*, savoury Greek appetizers, and the traditional *hamalia*, were being circulated by waiters drafted over from the hotel.

And the past was kaleidoscoping again. Alexandros Diamakis had been the only member of Yan's family to approve of their proposed marriage four years ago. In the brief lead-up to that long-ago cancelled wedding he'd been supportive and affectionate, in stark contrast to Sofia and her mother, Aunt Maria, and numerous other Diamakis and Theopolou relatives, who all seemed to be here this evening to celebrate Christophor's Name Day, bearing small gifts—beautiful little clothes for this new, unexpected addition to the family, sweets, or flowers.

Dark eyes, so like Yan's, so like Christophor's, were inspecting her fixed smile and tense appearance. Alexandros was in his mid-sixties, a tall, lean, upright figure of a man with a thick thatch of steel-grey hair and a compelling, hawkish face. Was this Yan in thirty years' time? she wondered abruptly. Still virile, still commanding?

'You look enchantingly glamorous, my dear,' he was saying, handing her a drink and admiring her outfit with a twinkle of humour. Eleanor smiled with a hint of apology. Tonight hadn't worked out at all as she'd expected. She'd gone into Skiathos Town earlier in the week with the express purpose of finding something worthy of this last night, something which would boost her shaky confidence under the unfriendly gaze of the Diamakis clan. She'd located an exclusive boutique, spent several thousand drachmas, and the result was a defiantly provocative sheath of scarlet silk, vaguely oriental in design, high at the front, plunging to a reckless V at the back, and slashed to mid-thigh on one side.

Not her usual choice of dress, she had to admit, but it summed up her image as she pictured it to be in the eyes of Yan's family.

With her newly acquired tan, her hair freshly washed and swinging loose and heavy down her back, discreet make-up and with bare feet pushed into elegant, high-heeled black suede court shoes, the look was glamorous, daringly vampish and remarkably eye-catching . . .

The only thing was, the gaze of the Diamakis clan seemed anything but unfriendly. In the four years since she'd seen them, either they'd mellowed out of all recognition, or she'd become a great deal less sensitive. Everyone she'd met during this happy celebration on the softly lit terrace at Yan's house had clutched her warmly by the hand, expressed what seemed to be genuine pleasure at seeing her here. In the defiant scarlet dress, she was beginning to feel rather foolish . . .

'I've been away,' Alexandros was saying, 'visiting some of my wife's relatives in England, and taking a look at Yan's new hotels at the same time. The first I heard of your return was two days ago. Yan rang me to invite me to come and say *chronia polla* to Christophor tonight . . .'

'My return?' she queried, with a faint blush. The remark about Yan's having new hotels in England had sent her brain into fresh reels of shock, but she was more concerned about the use of the word 'return'. It sounded too . . . final. Too permanent. She'd hate him to get the wrong impression. 'Didn't Yan tell you I'm leaving tomorrow?'

There was a short silence. The party swirled on around them, but Yan's father's dark eyes were clouded with concern as he concentrated all his attention on her.

'My dear girl, I thought that Yan...' There was a short, baffled silence. Then he said quietly, 'Eleanor, my dear, don't let my headstrong son push you into anything hasty...'

'Oh, he's not pushing me,' she retorted with a shaky laugh. Alexandros didn't know, she realised. Yan didn't appear to have told his father anything. Alexandros didn't understand...

Raking an unsteady hand through the thickness of her hair, she caught Aunt Maria's eyes across the crowded terrace. To her continued surprise, the older woman smiled and nodded, albeit rather cautiously.

I must be hallucinating, Eleanor decided wryly. Focusing on Alexandros again, she continued flatly, 'Yan's not pushing me. I'm going... I'm going because I have to...'

'I hope I'm not speaking out of turn,' said Alexandros quietly, 'but do you have any idea what it did to Yan when you left four years ago?'

'What it *did* to him?' She stared at him blankly. Where was Yan, anyway? Glancing distractedly round the crowds, she could see Christophor, darting excitedly between adult legs with Evangelie's niece and nephew. But Yan so far had been nowhere to be found. Nor had Sofia...

'He spent the first six months furiously obsessed with trying to trace you. It was only when your friend Laura told him the following summer that you were happily married to another man that he abandoned the quest.'

'Laura said that?' Eleanor's heart did a strange somersault in her chest. She blinked in growing confusion. 'I didn't tell her to say that...'

'Nevertheless, that is what she said. So you can imagine how Yan might have felt when you wrote, out of the blue, told him about his son?' Alexandros spoke with gentle urgency.

Shaking her head in slow denial, she began to speak, but he went on, 'Yan would no doubt wish to kill me if he knew I was interfering, Eleanor, my dear. Intense pride has always been his fatal flaw...'

'But he was engaged to marry Sofia. He didn't tell me!' she said in a low, defensive voice. 'He'd only offered to marry me because he knew I was pregnant...'

'My dear child, I think you either underestimate my son's intelligence, or you overestimate his sense of duty and honour...' Alexandros commented wryly.

'*Kalispera*, Father. Eleanor.' Yan's deep drawl made them both jump guiltily. Eleanor felt Yan's derisive gaze on her appearance as she turned to warily greet him. He was immaculate in a loose pale grey silk shirt, impeccably cut charcoal linen trousers, and a muted floral silk tie. Not for the first time that evening, she felt a twinge of regret at her defiant stance, wearing the brilliant, clinging red dress.

'Is this outfit intended to be symbolic, Eleanor? The scarlet woman, defying the disapproving family?'

The cruel accuracy of the taunt made it harder
to bear. Aghast, she felt her face warming to what
must be approaching the red of her dress.

'Not very chivalrous, Yannis,' his father re-
proved mildly. 'Eleanor's dress is guaranteed to
raise the temperature of every red-blooded male in
the room. It certainly has my vote.'

The light, humorous tone did little to lessen the
mounting tension.

'I am not blind.' Yan's retort was dry. 'Has my
father been harassing you about calling Christophor
Alexandros, to follow Greek tradition?'

'Why, no...' Eleanor stared from Yan to his
father in dawning realisation. Of course, the tradition. The first child was to be called after his
grandfather... She'd forgotten. 'I'm sorry,' she
said briefly, with a slightly anxious glance at
Alexandros. 'It wasn't an intentional snub or
anything...'

'My dear, don't give it a thought.' Alexandros
looked obliquely at his son. 'I was just about to
give your beautiful Eleanor a little advice about
something far more important...'

'Unfortunately, she is not *my* beautiful Eleanor.
She is planning to marry somebody else—a
psychopath called Geoffrey Terence-Evans.' The
clipped drawl betrayed Yan's suppressed emotions.

'A *homeopath*!' Eleanor snapped in a strained
voice.

'Ah, yes. A *homeopath*,' Yan agreed dismis-
sively, an unholy glitter in his eyes.

'Is this true?' Alexandros looked
slightly perplexed.

'Well...'

'I may be prejudiced, but my advice is to marry Yan, my dear. But don't let my son imagine for one minute that *he* is the boss. My marriage to my late wife Charlotte was a supremely happy one, but only when I'd learned who really wore the trousers in our house. Do you follow?'

'Father——' Yan appeared to have lost patience abruptly '—you are not yet in your dotage. Kindly refrain from meddling in things which do not concern you.'

'I have now refrained,' the older man announced good-humouredly, placing a hand on Yan's shoulder as he smiled at Eleanor. 'Excuse me, both of you; I think I saw Sofia arriving...'

Eleanor's eyes followed Alexandros's progress across the terrace, to where Sofia had appeared. She was curvaceously beautiful, as always, a glittery present in her hand, her red lips smiling. Eleanor watched Alexandros greet his stepniece and detain her beside him with what seemed to be a determined warmth and heartiness. Was he doing it deliberately? Steering Sofia away from Yan and herself? She stared at the girl, darkly exotic in black leggings and a diaphanous silver and white overblouse. Lashings of silver jewellery adorned her olive skin. Eleanor felt even more ridiculous in her 'scarlet woman' outfit. Her stomach clenched. She just wished this ordeal were over, that she could leave with Christophor...

Glancing up at Yan's inscrutable face, she said abruptly, 'I'd forgotten how much I liked your father.'

'I have always had the impression that the feeling was mutual,' Yan said flatly. His dark eyes roamed the length of her slender body in the red dress, his gaze kindling on the curves beneath the clinging silk. 'What a pity I have never achieved a similar level in your esteem.'

'I thought we'd agreed to stop bickering,' she reminded him acidly, 'to get this party over with, and then call it a day.'

'Is that what we agreed?' he murmured expressionlessly.

'You know damn well it is!'

'Hush, Eleanor,' he chided, sliding his arm round her waist in a lethally possessive fashion. 'For Christophor's sake, we should present a united front tonight. Don't you agree?'

'I...' Moistening her lips nervously, she fought down the panicky trickles of response to his touch.

'Of course you agree. You love Christophor, do you not?' The smile in his eyes was coolly heartless. He kept hold of her, forming them into what appeared to be an inseparable couple as Christophor came dancing up to see them.

'Mummy, Papa! My party's good! I've got *presents*!'

Without releasing her, Yan bent to scoop the small boy off the floor and into his other arm, settling him against his hip, smiling into the child's eyes.

'That's good. I'm glad you like your party! *Chronia polla*, little one. *Na ta ekatostisis*!'

'What does that mean, Papa?'

'It means, "Many happy returns", and "May you live one hundred years!"'

Eleanor cast a distraught glance around them. The three of them made an ironically idyllic family unit. This little performance seemed so genuine that she could almost forget her bitterness and her resolution, and play along with it for real.

Uncle Stefan, looking for all the world like a bandit in his best suit, was leading a growing line of dancers, arms linked, with much laughter and ribaldry between the men as they moved in the age-old Greek rhythms, sensual, dignified, graceful.

'Come and dance,' Yan ordered, with a gleam in his eyes. 'Do you still remember how to do this dance?'

'No, I've forgotten,' she said tightly.

'Then I shall teach you again...'

Caught up in the laughter, the rhythm of the music, the joy of Christophor's smile as he watched them, she felt her heart swelling almost unbearably with suppressed emotion. Around them, darkness was falling. In the warm summer night, with the floodlights in the cypress trees, there was the sharp smell of pine and the heady sweetness of flowers. Behind the white walls of Yan's villa the sky filled with stars, one by one, dropping from infinity.

Sofia was watching the dancing. Catching the Greek girl's grey stare, Eleanor saw bitter fury. The glimpse jolted her. Surely Sofia would be triumphant, knowing that her much despised rival had opted to leave tomorrow? The hostile gaze made her even more uneasy. When the dance came to an end, and broke up in laughing disarray, she began to detach herself from Yan, turning to find some excuse to escape. But as she opened her mouth to speak to him, he bent his head and kissed her, hard and long.

Trapped in the double-edged situation, she could only freeze and endure it. Yan caught her closer, running lean hands along the silky length of her back, then around beneath her armpits to skim the sides of her breasts. She caught her breath in a muffled gasp of shock.

'It's been a strain, this last few days,' he murmured laughingly against her cheek, 'keeping my hands off you...'

'You've always got Sofia to...to *grope*!' she spat, through smiling lips.

'But I do not wish to "grope" Sofia,' he teased darkly, pinning her at his side. 'And such inelegant phrases do you no justice, Eleanor.'

'It's getting late,' she countered shakily, wishing that her pulses would slow down, that her heart would stop thudding at his nearness. 'I should get Christophor to bed.'

'I will help...'

'*No*!' The refusal was jerked out. 'Yan, please...you've had your...your pound of flesh. I've stayed until tonight; I've...I've kept my side of the bargain. Now...please...*please*...just leave me *alone*!'

Yan let his hands drop from her. He stood very still, his eyes shadowed. His face was dark and expressionless.

'Eleanor, can't you understand?' There was a trace of suppressed anger in his deep voice. 'You don't have to go. I don't want you to go.'

'I *have* to go. Goodbye, Yan,' she whispered chokingly.

His mouth hardened, the lines from nose to mouth deepening with grim, proud hostility, but he said nothing. The dark gaze locked searchingly, bitterly with hers. It seemed to drill right inside her head. Did he *know* how torn apart she was feeling? With a slight sob, she turned away from that ruthless, hawk-like appraisal, pushed through the crowd, and went blindly in search of Christophor, her throat so tight and choked that she could hardly speak.

Bath and bedtime, even with Evangelie's help, seemed the hardest work she'd ever done. Her nerves were so on edge that she jumped violently when there was a tap on her bedroom door shortly after she'd tucked Christophor up and switched off his light. Yan. Was it Yan, come to make a last-ditch effort to persuade her to stay? Her stomach tightened. Heart drumming, she opened the door with a trembling hand.

Sofia stood there. The glitter in her grey eyes seemed very bright, almost feverish.

'Sofia?' Eleanor was wearily polite. 'Did you want something?'

'No. Only to check that you are all packed up, and leaving in the morning.'

Eleanor felt her cheeks darken.

'Yes, I am,' she retorted shortly. 'Is that all?'

'Yes...except that Yan asked me to give you this,' Sofia said softly, reaching into her pocket. '*Adio*, Eleanor. Have a *safe* trip back to England.'

With a surge of angry disbelief, Eleanor watched as the Greek girl produced her passport, with a flourish, and handed it to her with smug satisfaction.

CHAPTER NINE

THE flight was called. A jittery surge of adrenalin followed her progress through Passport Control, through the baggage checks, through the departure lounge, and out on to the air-strip.

Eleanor glanced down at Christophor's shiny dark head as he trotted along beside her, in his bright red cotton shorts and T-shirt, then cast a last glance back at the airport building, already shimmering like a mirage in the heatwaves rising from the hot concrete. She'd won. She'd forced Yan to let her go, let her leave Greece with his beloved Christophor. So why wasn't she feeling relieved? Elated, even?

As farewell parties went, she reflected numbly, last night's had been unforgettable. This morning she should be feeling liberated, victorious, free... Yan had kept his promise. He'd let her go. So why did she feel so on edge, so strung up?

Maybe it was just that she couldn't trust him yet. Maybe this open-handed generosity of Yan's, connected with his son's future, was hard to believe. It was just too good to be true. Would she only feel truly relieved, truly *free* of his possessiveness and tyranny, when she was actually stepping off the plane in London, with Christophor safely back on home soil...?

'Will Papa come to see us soon?' Christophor, probably after his late night and their early getaway this morning, seemed fractious and miserable.

'Of course, sweetheart ...' This tension was unbearable, she decided. Chewing her lower lip, she smoothed nervously damp palms over the neat severity of her glossy brown French plait, and down the skirt of her china-blue and cream linen suit...

To minimise the endless travelling for Christophor they were spending the night in London with a friend, before catching the train up to Newcastle the next day. There wasn't a single reason for a last-minute hitch in her escape... The reassurances ran silently through her head.

What if Yan appeared at the airport before the flight took off? What if he'd somehow managed to produce some legal complication, which he'd kept quiet until the eleventh hour? What if he could legally snatch Christophor from her?

He loved Christophor so much that he was probably capable of anything. If she hadn't already realised how much from every action and every word she'd witnessed since arriving in Skiathos, she was left in no doubt by the way he'd said goodbye to him last night. If Yan had ever spoken to her like that, if he'd vowed always to love her, more than anyone else, to be always there for her, the way he'd huskily told Christophor... She bit her lip hard, tasting blood.

Instead, Yan Diamakis's interest in her had finished the way it had started—only in physical desire.

She shivered convulsively. That last, roughly branding kiss in front of everyone at the party, the

possessive light in his gaze as he'd abruptly released her ... Did he have any idea how desperately
she'd wanted to respond? How deeply she loved
him, in spite of everything ...?

The adrenalin surging through her veins sub-
sided a fraction as she reached the foot of the re-
tractable metal steps up to the aircraft. It faded still
more as she found her seat, and Christophor's. It
diminished even further as she slotted her hand
luggage in the overhead locker.

It finally vanished as she sat down and assessed
the fact that they were really free to go, that no one
appeared to be about to stop her taking her son and
flying out of Greece with him, back home to
England ...

With the 'fight or flight' reflex gone, Eleanor felt
strangely deflated: empty, and disturbingly un-
certain about her victory. When she closed her eyes
it wasn't Yan's bitter mockery, or the humiliation
of Sofia's handing her the passport, which swam
into her mind. The image was Yan's face, harsh
with pride and pain, as she walked away from him.
And the other image was the warmth, the love and
joy generated at that party. The very opposite to
the atmosphere she'd been fearing ...

A family pushed past them, two small children
excitedly jumping on to their seats, the wife ex-
changing humorous glances of resignation with her
husband as he stowed their baggage above. A
family. Together. Sharing things; a secure unit.
Didn't Christophor deserve at least a chance at that
sort of childhood?

The empty sensation intensified.

For some inexplicable reason, now that escape seemed within her grasp, all the fierce determination to leave seemed to be abruptly metamorphosing into an acute attack of conscience... Her emotions see-sawed wildly. *Was* the prospect of staying here in Greece with Yan so unthinkable...? Was it?

His words came back to haunt her. 'You don't have to go', he'd said. 'I don't want you to go'...

Her heart twisted in anguished uncertainty. Yan might not love her, but he adored his son. Wasn't she strong enough to give it a chance, let Yan try and prove his commitment to making a family for Christophor?

There was Sofia... but, although Sofia's parting shot had hurt, Eleanor found she was suddenly facing a fresh perspective on that, too. Could she really believe Sofia? Didn't Yan's fury with Sofia at the Theopolou taverna make it hard to believe he'd entrusted the girl with delivering the passport...? Wasn't it rather more likely that Yan's sweet-natured stepcousin had been stirring up trouble again—found the passport, jumped at the chance of a final malicious flourish?

The logical, sensible thoughts crowded in, making her feel dizzy, making her head spin...

Glancing back at the airport, at the shimmer of heat haze, the truth hit her without warning. With cold certainty. With the clarity of a revelation. She was wrong. So wrong. So unfair on Christophor. She was being immature, idealistic. She was being proud, selfish and over-romantic. Letting her mother's experience with her errant father colour her emotions. Letting pride and fear rule her decision...

Her stomach churning with nerves and apprehension, her heart suddenly thumping as if she'd run a race, she stood up, trembling violently, retrieving her baggage, extricating an increasingly irritable Christophor from his intent labours to fasten his own safety-belt, pushing past the queue of other passengers still boarding, explaining, apologising in fractured panic to the stunned air hostess. The whole thing seemed to happen in distraught slow motion, like the crucial scene from some suspense film.

'Are we going back to see Papa?' Christophor demanded. He was glaring up at her. The look in his eyes reminded her so forcibly of Yan that she managed a shaky smile.

'Yes,' she admitted chokingly, taking a deep steadying breath to control her scattered nerves. 'Yes, we are. We're going back to see your papa...'

The villa was deserted when they got back. No Evangelie, no Yan. Heart in mouth, Eleanor left her luggage on the terrace, and nervously scanned the garden and beach. There was no one in sight.

Out in the bay, skimming in the wake of a powerful launch, a lone figure was water-skiing. Slowly she and Christophor went down the garden, and on to the hot, empty beach. She stood in the shade of the pines, shielding her eyes, as the water-skier arced in closer, travelling at a reckless speed which made her breathless. There was an unmistakable style, a kind of ferocious grace, about the man's movements. Yan. Her heart skipped and plunged. Here she was, earnestly returning, full of anguished self-denial. And there was Yan, blithely water-skiing, as if he didn't have a care in the world . . .

Bitter self-mockery rippled through her. Yan didn't even care that she'd gone. She should have taken her chance of escape. She should have stayed on the plane . . .

As the launch pulled closer to shore he skidded off the shallows, and on to the sand, as effortlessly as a circus athlete. But when she stepped from the shade and lifted a hand to hail him, he froze into stillness.

'Eleanor?' The exclamation was husky, disbelieving.

'Papa!' Uninhibited by tension, Christophor broke away from her to run and greet him, and was swept into his father's arms. The reunion was painful to watch, but drummed home her dogged line in unselfish good sense. The sins of the fathers, she thought stubbornly. And also of the mothers. Her romantic folly had led to her son's conception. She had to admit it now. And she'd always thought that old adage so terribly unfair . . .

'Eleanor?' He was striding towards her up the beach, glistening dark gold in the sunlight, magnificent as a sun-god in his own private kingdom. Yan's narrowed gaze revealed such a degree of cautious brilliance that she felt her stern self-control crumbling.

'Hello, Yan,' she managed weakly, swallowing on her paper-dry throat.

'Papa, teach me to do that?' Christophor was saying, pointing out to the bay where the launch idled, the driver and another man from the watersports club lazing on deck, watching them.

'Perhaps. In a short while, little one. First I think your mother and I...need to talk.'

He gazed at her quizzically. That initial glitter of emotion she'd seen had been ruthlessly extinguished. The coolly ironic mask was back.

'Well?'

'I...we came back,' she explained shortly. For the life of her, now that she was back here on the beach, facing Yan, she couldn't even begin to think how to explain her sudden attack of logic and fairness on the plane, her noble motives for returning.

'I can see that.' His deep voice was dry. 'Did you forget something again? Not your passport, I trust.'

'I...no. I didn't forget anything.' This was excruciating. Worse than she'd dreamed. She stared at his lean, pitilessly strong physique, the ripple of muscle in thigh and abdomen. In the brief dark tan swimming-trunks, his black hair wet and slicked back, he exuded such an ominous air of cool authority that she quaked inwardly. Was he going to make her *crawl* back, beg him to renew his cynical offer of marriage? Was she going to be able to go through with this ordeal, after all?

'Then perhaps you'd like to explain?'

'Can we go somewhere more...private?' she said tautly.

She was dying inside. She wanted to scream with frustration and uncertainty.

'Endaxi.' He nodded stiffly, turning to shout something in Greek to the men on the boat, and placing Christophor down on the sand. 'Come up to the house.'

The launch had nosed in closer, and Yan waded back to retrieve denims, black espadrilles and a cream cotton shirt, extracting a bunch of keys from the pocket as he roughly dragged the clothes on.

'I will ring Evangelie,' he said shortly as they trooped into the cool, tiled hall. 'She will come and take charge of Christophor...'

The housekeeper arrived within five minutes of the call. The idea of saying hello again to his small friends thankfully appealed to Christophor's bewildered emotions. Fortified with fruit juice and biscuits, he consented quite happily to being whisked off to Evangelie's sister's house in the village.

'That leaves you and me, Eleanor,' Yan commented flatly, bringing a tray of coffee out on to the terrace and setting it down on the cane table. 'So start explaining.'

'Do I need to explain?' she snapped, her overstrung nerves close to breaking. 'Do you have to be so obtuse, Yan? Can't you smell *victory* when it's sitting right under your arrogant nose?'

'Victory?' The word was very quiet, and bitter. 'In what sense do I smell victory, Eleanor?'

'Oh, for the love of God! You wanted me to marry you, for Christophor's sake. Here I am. I'll marry you, if you still want me...'

There was a charged, almost electric silence. Inside she was hurting so much that she fantasised she might almost be bleeding to death with pain and fear of rejection.

'Well?' she whispered raggedly. 'Do you?'

Yan's face had darkened, hardened to such grim, muted anger that she hardly recognised him. The brilliant gaze raked her slender figure, from the top of her shiny French plait, over her steady, intense jade gaze, down over her floral blue and cream suit, bare brown legs and low tan leather sandals.

'What made you change your mind?' he queried softly.

'The ... the fact that you let me go? With Christophor?'

'*What*?'

'I ... it's true.' She nodded, with a husky, nervous laugh. 'I think what frightened me most was the idea that you'd never let Christophor leave. That you'd pull any stunt to keep him here in Greece ...'

A hard smile twitched at the corners of his mouth.

'That is close to the truth.'

'And yet you let me take him. I ... I was on the plane. And suddenly I knew I really was free to go, and ...'

'And suddenly you didn't want to go any more?' Yan finished up for her scathingly. 'What if I have changed my mind, my sweet Eleanor?'

Fear rose up inside her, expanding like a physical ball of pain.

'Yan ...'

'What if I am no longer interested in your supreme sacrifice—the martyrdom of your real wishes and emotions, for the sake of our son?'

She stared at him, aghast.

'I thought you *loved* Christophor!'

'I do. More than this air I breathe,' Yan affirmed shortly. 'But perhaps my pride is greater than I thought. I am no longer sure I could face the rest of my days with a wife who sees me as the lowest form of human life.'

She felt the heat rush to her face and neck.

'Yan, I thought the overriding concern was for Christophor?' she persisted quietly. 'If I'm prepared to enter into a marriage without . . . without love, for his sake, then surely . . .'

'Not your marriage of convenience again,' he jeered softly. 'If we marry, Eleanor, it would be marriage in the fullest sense.'

'Yes. I know . . .' She was burning all over with mortification.

'You expect me to happily share your bed? And imagine that you are pining after this man called Geoffrey Terence-Evans every night, wishing it were he making love to you again?'

'But I don't love Geoffrey!'

'Then why were you about to marry him?'

'I wasn't.' The heat intensified under the black stare. 'I . . . I used the fact that he's proposed to me many times as . . . as self-defence. As for wishing it were he making love to me again, that's hardly likely. Because he never has.'

Yan regarded her in unrelenting silence.

'You do not have to lie to me about moral rectitude,' he said at last, his tone jeeringly abrasive. 'I am not a puritan. Nor am I that blinkered chauvinist you so firmly believe me to be. A woman can desire a man, just as a man can desire a woman.'

'I'm not lying. Geoffrey has been a good friend. We've gone out for... for meals, to cinemas, theatres, things like that. But to tell you the total truth, there's been no one since you...'

'You expect me to believe that?'

'Believe what you like.' It was no good, she thought despairingly. What a fool she was, coming back for more. She could have been winging her way to London, right this minute. Slow-burning anger and indignation took over from fear and embarrassment.

'Yan, I'm trying to be *honest*. And the reason...' She wavered, gathered courage. 'The reason I came back, if you really must know, is that I *love* you!'

Her words fell into the tense silence, and her heart squeezed in her chest.

'God only knows why!' she ploughed on doggedly. 'But I love you. So it's not just for Christophor. It's for me. Because I... I don't think that I can go home to England, and start up my normal life again, knowing how much you still mean to me...'

She caught a ragged breath, her eyes blazing into his impassive stare.

'So don't talk to me about pride, Yan! There's mine gone—trampled on the floor under your damned feet!'

Yan's face was paler beneath his tan. His mouth was grim, his eyes haggard.

'We can still take a later flight,' she whispered, with fierce defensiveness. She stood up, on legs which felt like cotton wool. Turning blindly away, she heard Yan say something harshly indecipherable under his breath. With a grating of his chair on the terrace tiles he stood up too. With an abrupt jerk of his hand, he reached for her and pulled her back, holding her tightly by the upper arms.

'Eleanor...?' His deep voice was rough, unsteady. 'Eleanor, you would not lie to me again? Is it true that you love me?'

'Of course it's true, you stupid idiot!' she blazed at him, tears stinging her eyelids.

His face twisted with bleak humour.

'Is this how you see the man you love? As a stupid idiot?'

'Yes! And worse! You're...you're proud, arrogant, domineering, cruel, heartless...'

She was shuddering in his merciless grip.

'Enough. There is only so much flattery I can take, little one...'

'What's even worse—even worse than your mockery and your cynicism and your patronising sense of humour—is you don't even have the courage to tell me whether or not *you* love *me*!' she finished up, on a rush of breathless fury.

Yan regarded her gravely for a few seconds, shaking his head slowly, like a man awakening from a trance.

'Then pride is my greatest evil,' he breathed unsteadily. 'Because I have loved you so deeply, for so long, sweet Eleanor, I have hardly slept one night without thinking of you.'

'How can you say that when you've never, ever told me before?'

A gleam of amusement warmed his eyes again.

'How can I follow your supreme logic, Eleanor?'

'Don't mock me!'

'I am not mocking you, my darling.' The endearment caught her breath, made her heart swell without warning… 'I am mocking myself. If I have never said the words, blame cowardice, fear, pride… I am all those things you've called me. But believe me, I love you.'

'Truly?' Joy was creeping cautiously from behind its barriers. The smile she turned up to him was luminous with hope.

'Do not doubt me,' he warned grimly, tightening his hold so cruelly that she was crushed into his body, from breast to thigh. The tight contact was igniting a slow-burning fire which seemed to flicker from deep in her secret centre.

'Then tell me again… and again… and again!' A warm, soft cloud of wonder and happiness was floating somewhere just beneath her feet…

'I love you,' he groaned with soft savagery. 'S'agapó, Eleanor. And se thélo, I want you. I have been burning for you this last week, too proud to touch you again until last night, when I knew that you were going…'

'Oh, Yan…' The warm cloud had risen in temperature. The heat was a furnace, consuming her in its white-hot fire. 'I want you, too…' She was hot, but shivering inside, like a fever…

'Then there is only one remedy,' he whispered, bending to lift her into his arms and carry her inside, and up to his room.

'And what's that?' she teased daringly, flushed and trembling as he laid her, with a flourish, like a pirate's prize in the centre of his bed. 'A massage, perhaps? With ylang-ylang and sandalwood, for arousing the senses?'

'My senses need no arousing, my darling. They are about to explode.' His voice was slightly unsteady, his amused eyes very intent as he dispensed with his shirt and came down beside her to unbutton the blouse of her linen suit painstakingly, dropping a kiss on each freshly exposed oval of flesh, until she was squirming with impatience. 'Later, Eleanor, we need to straighten things out between us. Right now I cannot think straight for wanting to do this... and this...'

'Oh, Yan... please...!' She was breathless with pleasure.

'And this...'

Every agonising second of the last few days, every frustrated moment of misery and longing, seemed to erupt into tempestuous passion. In their agony of impatience, buttons ripped and clothes were tossed anyhow. Half laughing, half crying, she forgot time, place, everything else, every atom of her body focused on this glorious union, the relentless build-up of pleasure, the need and love between them stronger than she'd ever known. When the exquisite explosion shook her violently, igniting the fathoms-deep mystery inside her, she convulsed against Yan's hard body and clung to him like a survivor from an earthquake...

'*Eleanor*...!' The disbelieving groan was ripped from Yan as he savagely crushed her to him. 'How could you ever have doubted that I loved you?'

She stayed quiet for long enough to slow her breathing, to reassemble her senses in some kind of random order. Then, holding tightly to the iron-hard arms enclosing her, she said slowly, 'Because you never told me.'

'You needed to hear the words?' he quizzed hoarsely. 'Did my actions not speak louder than any words, my sweet Eleanor?'

'Maybe. But do you remember that first time...? I blurted out my love for you. You never said it back. Never...'

'And you never said it again,' he pointed out, his dark eyes gleaming with laughter. 'So I discounted it as a romantic aberration, something an innocent little *parthénos* might say in the heat of the moment, and then regret...'

'Oh, Yan...!'

'I spent my whole summer with you, *agapití mou*!' he reminded her with justice. 'Every free waking hour. I wanted to keep you with me forever. But you were so young...'

'Too young to tell me you loved me?'

'I loved you,' he assured her wryly, his eyes suddenly very bright and level beneath heavy lids. 'I loved you the moment I saw you that first evening, sitting on the beach, staring at me with that fresh, wide-eyed innocence...'

He caressed her with hungry intimacy, from groin to breast, kissing her neck and feeling her convulsive shiver of response with a low groan of desire. 'And I must confess I was frightened...'

'Frightened? Of me?'

'Frightened of the way you made me feel. To love someone is to feel vulnerable. And after the pressure from Sofia and the family, I was feeling...cautious. Wary of rushing into total commitment...'

'Tell me about Sofia.' She stirred in his arms, twisting to look into the dark brilliance of his eyes.

'I told you before. The family—at least her side of the family—were very anxious to see us marry...'

'So...you were *pushed* into getting engaged to her?' Eleanor ventured hesitantly. Somehow she found it impossible to imagine Yan being pushed into anything...

'In truth, after the shock of my mother's death, I was in a kind of limbo for months. The family was pressing for this closer tie between the two branches. Sofia had made no secret of her... infatuation for me...'

He felt her tense slightly, and tightened his arms around her. 'Losing my mother had left the family feeling torn apart. I wasn't sure if I'd ever feel any emotion again. It seemed the right thing to do. It wasn't until I met you that I realised I'd been only half awake. I broke off my involvement with Sofia before you and I first made love,' he reminded her quietly.

'You didn't tell me you'd been engaged to her...'

'I didn't feel that concerned you.' He shot her a wry smile. 'And yes, Eleanor, I know that proves that I am arrogant, domineering, all those things you say I am...'

'Finish telling me about Sofia,' she urged softly, reaching to twine her arms round his neck.

'She found it...hard to accept. I did not feel proud of myself. My only defence was that perhaps I was not in my right mind when the liaison was suggested. She was going away to the family's house in Tuscany for the summer. I think she expected me to have changed my mind, that my brief affair with this young English girl would have fizzled out... The night she got back, she met me in the beach bar by the hotel. When she discovered that I was still involved with you, and considering asking you to marry me, she was very upset...'

Eleanor drew back a little to see his face.

'You were going to ask me to marry you? Before you knew about the baby?'

'Oh, yes, Eleanor.' Yan's voice was hoarse with wry self-mockery. 'But I was frightened. Just as I said. Wary of another commitment, so soon after the mistaken one with Sofia. And then your friend—your colleague Laura—appeared. She saw me with Sofia. She came over to inform me that I was a two-timing bastard, and that you were expecting my child. She would have done better to tell me in private, not in front of Sofia. Knowing you were pregnant gave Sofia the ammunition to launch her offensive. She saw a way to undermine your confidence. After that, it didn't matter what I said. You were determined to doubt my motives...'

Eleanor nodded slightly, with a shiver of remorse. So *that* was how Sofia had known, so quickly, about Eleanor's pregnancy. Laura was well-meaning, but she had difficulty keeping her own counsel about anything. All this time she'd believed that Yan had told Sofia. That had hurt. The idea that he'd told Sofia her secret, confided in Sofia his reason for proposing marriage...

'Laura didn't say Sofia was with you. But I knew she'd told you I was pregnant. I was so angry with her, I could have strangled her...'

There was a moment's silence.

'Would you not have told me, Eleanor?' There was a strained note in Yan's voice. 'About the baby?'

'Yes. I would have told you. But in my own good time. I was frightened too—frightened of rejection. Once a girl tells a man she's pregnant, it looks as if she's trying to...to trap him into marriage. I wanted to be sure you wouldn't be thoroughly embarrassed and run a mile.'

'How you underestimate me.'

'That's what your father said last night.'

'I had the feeling the old devil was meddling.' There was affectionate warmth in Yan's voice, belying the caustic words.

'Which reminds me... Why didn't you tell me you tried to find me?' she demanded suddenly, sitting up to face Yan with a reproachful frown. 'And another thing...why didn't you tell me you had business ventures and hotels in England?'

'Hold on a minute; slow down. One accusation at a time, please.'

She had to smile at the gleam of laughter in Yan's eyes.

'The answer to the first question is that my pride had been dented sufficiently. Leaving me a curt note saying you were no longer pregnant, that it had been a big mistake, disappearing without any address ... Do you think I wanted you gloating that I'd spent the next six months obsessively trying to find you? Do you imagine I could face the thought of you jeering about that, too?'

'*Jeering*? Yan, I would never have——'

'And then Laura told me, the following summer, when I asked her if she knew where you were. You were married, she said. Happily married. That was when I called off my search.'

'Oh, Yan...' Laura—meddlesome, well-meaning, over-zealous Laura—had a lot to answer for, she reflected with a twist of rueful anger.

'We could invite her to our wedding, and supply a gag?' Yan's suggestion was deadpan.

Giggling, she reached to kiss him again, felt the fierce hunger of his response as he ran possessive hands the length of her spine, fenced tongues with hers, pushed her back against the softness of the bed, and began the whole blissful cycle of desire all over again. For a long while, further coherent conversation was impossible.

Much, much later, she stirred in the warm security of his arms.

'You look like a sleepy kitten,' Yan murmured teasingly, his dark eyes moving over her body with a fierce tenderness which contracted her heart with happiness.

'When I came back, and saw you water-skiing, I thought you were a heartless brute.'

'I might have promised, on my honour, to let you go——' he made the confession ruefully '—but I was fighting the humiliating urge to jump in the jeep and intercept you at the airport. Water-skiing at high speed seemed the best therapy...'

'I forgive you...' Another thought occurred to her. '*Did* you ask Sofia to bring my passport back to me last night?'

Yan expelled his breath on a sudden, abrupt sigh.

'What do *you* think?'

Eleanor began to laugh softly in his arms. 'I decided while I was sitting on the plane that, although you *might* have been feeling extra spiteful, it was actually far more likely that Sofia decided to stage one last, dramatic sour grapes.'

She felt Yan relax. 'Thank God you have suddenly seen the light,' he said drily. 'She found it on my desk at the hotel. I'd been intending to give it to you first thing this morning...'

'Leaving it until the eleventh hour?' she teased, loving him so much that she felt she might burst...

'Of course. I wanted another excuse to see you, convince you that you were making a mistake...'

'Which I was,' she cut in happily.

'Which you were,' he agreed. 'Persuading you to stay for Christophor's Name Day was another ruse. I wanted to show you how much the family supported us. And I wanted to demonstrate to Sofia my total commitment to you and my child...'

'Oh, Yan...'

'And just before we drop the subject of Sofia for good, let me put one last thing straight. Getting Sofia pregnant and feeling forced to propose marriage was never on the cards, my darling. I'm not that irresponsible. The only woman I've ever been so blindly carried away with was you. I wanted you so much that night that precautions were simply not an option...'

She gazed at him, warmth creeping into her cheeks.

'Truly?'

'Truly.' The blaze of emotion in his eyes took her breath away.

'Do you forgive me for not trusting you?' she whispered, her eyes glowing with happiness.

His reply was to kiss her with a mounting hunger which blotted out any lingering doubt.

'I've just thought,' she said, after another breathless interlude which rendered speech unnecessary, 'my luggage has gone to London. All I've got to wear is the suit I was travelling in... And what about Christophor...?'

'No problem. We'll go shopping. Or, better still, you can stay in bed with me until your luggage returns.' Yan laughed, hauling her roughly beneath him and triggering another set of delicious sensations in the process.

'You know how I used to love Greek myths and legends?' she managed, a trifle shakily.

'How could I forget?'

'Did you know that Apollo's temple at Delphi, surrounded by sheer mountains, was considered by the Greeks to be the centre of the earth?'

'Am I not Greek?' he teased. 'Do you imagine I am ignorant of the mythology of my own country?'

'Well, maybe that's why you put me in mind of Apollo,' she teased with a soft laugh, 'not because of the nymph Daphne story at all. For two more reasons. First, because with your... your aloof moods and your unreadable expressions you seemed as inaccessible as sheer mountains...'

'I... inaccessible?' He was caressing her upper arm rhythmically, his fingers brushing her breast, stoking the fires unbearably. 'You have total access to me, sweet Eleanor. Never forget it...'

'And second, you're the centre of my universe...' she finished up on a loving whisper.

'The centre of your universe?' The tenderness in the dark gaze flipped her heart over as he smoothed the damp brown hair from her flushed face, gently kissed her forehead. 'Am I, Eleanor?'

'Oh, yes,' she assured him gravely, her eyes dancing. 'And what's more, the Apollo legends might be impressive, but, where my future husband is concerned, I promise you, darling, no mere *legend* could even begin to compare...'

THREE TIMES
A LOVE STORY

A special collection of three individual love stories from one of the world's best-loved romance authors. This beautiful volume offers a unique chance for new fans to sample some of Janet Dailey's earlier works and for long-time fans to collect an edition to treasure.

W●RLDWIDE

AVAILABLE NOW   PRICED £4.99

Available from WH Smith, John Menzies, Volume One, Forbuoys, Martins, Woolworths, Tesco, Asda, Safeway and other paperback stockists. Also available from Worldwide Reader Service, FREEPOST, PO Box 236, Croydon, Surrey CR9 9EL. (UK Postage & Packing free)

MILLS & BOON

HEARTS OF FIRE by Miranda Lee

Welcome to our compelling family saga set in the glamorous world of opal dealing in Australia. Laden with dark secrets, forbidden desires and scandalous discoveries, **Hearts of Fire** unfolds over a series of 6 books, but each book also features a passionate romance with a happy ending and can be read independently.

Book 1: SEDUCTION & SACRIFICE
Published: April 1994   *FREE* with Book 2

WATCH OUT for special promotions!

Lenore had loved Zachary Marsden secretly for years. Loyal, handsome and protective, Zachary was the perfect husband. Only Zachary would never leave his wife…would he?

Book 2: DESIRE & DECEPTION
Published: April 1994   Price £2.50

Jade had a name for Kyle Armstrong: *Mr Cool.* He was the new marketing manager at Whitmore Opals—the job *she* coveted. However, the more she tried to hate this usurper, the more she found him attractive…

Book 3: PASSION & THE PAST
Published: May 1994   Price £2.50

Melanie was intensely attracted to Royce Grantham—which shocked her! She'd been so sure after the tragic end of her marriage that she would never feel for any man again. How strong was her resolve not to repeat past mistakes?

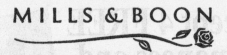

MILLS & BOON

HEARTS OF FIRE by Miranda Lee

Book 4: FANTASIES & THE FUTURE
Published: June 1994   Price £2.50

The man who came to mow the lawns was more stunning than any of Ava's fantasies, though she realised that Vincent Morelli thought she was just another rich, lonely housewife looking for excitement! But, Ava knew that her narrow, boring existence was gone forever...

Book 5: SCANDALS & SECRETS
Published: July 1994   Price £2.50

Celeste Campbell had lived on her hatred of Byron Whitmore for twenty years. Revenge was sweet...until news reached her that Byron was considering remarriage. Suddenly she found she could no longer deny all those long-buried feelings for him...

Book 6: MARRIAGE & MIRACLES
Published: August 1994   Price £2.50

Gemma's relationship with Nathan was in tatters, but her love for him remained intact—she was going to win him back! Gemma knew that Nathan's terrible past had turned his heart to stone, and she was asking for a miracle. But it was possible that one could happen, wasn't it?

Don't miss all six books!

Available from WH Smith, John Menzies, Volume One, Forbuoys, Martins, Woolworths, Tesco, Asda, Safeway and other paperback stockists. Also available from Mills & Boon Reader Service, FREEPOST, PO Box 236, Croydon, Surrey CR9 9EL (UK Postage & Packing free).

Accept 4 FREE Romances and 2 FREE gifts

FROM READER SERVICE

Here's an irresistible invitation from Mills & Boon. Please accept our offer of 4 FREE Romances, a CUDDLY TEDDY and a special MYSTERY GIFT! Then, if you choose, go on to enjoy 6 captivating Romances every month for just £1.90 each, postage and packing FREE. Plus our FREE Newsletter with author news, competitions and much more.

**Send the coupon below to:
Mills & Boon Reader Service,
FREEPOST, PO Box 236,
Croydon, Surrey CR9 9EL.**

NO STAMP REQUIRED

Yes! Please rush me 4 FREE Romances and 2 FREE gifts! Please also reserve me a Reader Service subscription. If I decide to subscribe I can look forward to receiving 6 brand new Romances for just £11.40 each month, post and packing FREE. If I decide not to subscribe I shall write to you within 10 days - I can keep the free books and gifts whatever I choose. I may cancel or suspend my subscription at any time. I am over 18 years of age.

Ms/Mrs/Miss/Mr _____ EP70R

Address _____

_____

Postcode _____ Signature _____

Offer closes 31st October 1994. The right is reserved to refuse an application and change the terms of this offer. One application per household. Offer not valid for current subscribers to this series. Valid in UK and Eire only. Overseas readers please write for details. Southern Africa write to IBS Private Bag X3010, Randburg 2125. You may be mailed with offers from other reputable companies as a result of this application. Please tick box if you would prefer not to receive such offers ☐